A SACK *of* TEETH

A SACK *of* TEETH

GRANT BUDAY

RAINCOAST BOOKS

Vancouver

Raincoast Books acknowledges the ongoing financial support of the Government of Canada through The Canada Council for the Arts and the Book Publishing Industry Development Program (BPIDP); and the Government of British Columbia through the BC Arts Council.

This is a work of fiction. Any resemblance to persons living or dead is coincidental.

Text design by Ingrid Paulson
Typeset by Teresa Bubela

NATIONAL LIBRARY OF CANADA CATALOGUING IN PUBLICATION DATA
Buday, Grant, 1956–
    A sack of teeth

ISBN 1-55192-457-9

    I. Title.
PS8553.U444S22 2002   C813'.54   C2001-911681-0
PR9199.3.B7636S22 2002

Library of Congress Control Number: 2002102367

Raincoast Books   In the United States:
9050 Shaughnessy Street   Publishers Group West
Vancouver, British Columbia   1700 Fourth Street
Canada   V6P 6E5   Berkeley, California
www.raincoast.com   94710

At Raincoast Books we are committed to protecting the environment and to the responsible use of natural resources. We are acting on this commitment by working with suppliers and printers to phase out our use of paper produced from ancient forest. This book is one step towards that goal. It is printed on 100% ancient-forest-free paper (100% post-consumer recycled), processed chlorine- and acid-free, and supplied by New Leaf Paper. It is printed with vegetable-based inks. For further information, visit our website at www.raincoast.com. We are working with Markets Initiative (www.oldgrowthfree.com) on this project.

Printed in Canada by Friesens

1 2 3 4 5 6 7 8 9 10

For Sam

Contents

No one told him he'd have to know things.

Prologue

At six years old, Jack Klein knew many things: that plums and apples tasted best when stolen, that by putting hockey gloves on your feet you become King Kong, and that the air in the freezer smelled like snow. He also knew that today was Labour Day, 1965. Labour Day was a holiday.

Summer was over; it hadn't rained for weeks in Vancouver and the grass was crisp underfoot. Jack had watched worms writhe on the sidewalks and seen families leave their doors wide for a sea breeze from Burrard Inlet. His dad said you could smell the rendering plant where they turned animals into lard.

The lead story on the TV news this Monday evening concerned former Nazi Albert Schell, found living right here in Vancouver.

Sixteen years working as a saw filer in a plywood mill. A neighbour scratched his crewcut and shrugged, saying Schell had canvassed for the Save the Children's Fund. At the commercial break BC Lions quarterback Joe Kapp — who had led the team to Grey Cup victory last fall — grinned, displaying teeth like a Buick's grille as he urged the kids to eat Squirrel peanut butter. But Jack Klein was not eating Squirrel, or drinking Goofy Grape, or chewing Dubble Bubble. He was across the alley visiting Ivor Skog. Jack and Ivor spent their days in the spell of childhood, cashing in pop bottles, smoking cigarette butts and following the railway tracks all the way to the waterfront where spooked gulls swirled like snow. Tomorrow, Jack would begin Grade One at Sir Horace Walpole Elementary. Nine-year-old Ivor was also starting Grade One — for the third time. At the moment, however, Jack and Ivor were not playing King Kong, stealing plums or wandering the railroad tracks. Right now Jack was inside a suitcase.

PART ONE

BEFORE SCHOOL

I

Burnt Lips

The suitcase stank of earwax. Jack's head, torso and right foot were crammed inside it, with only his left foot sticking out. He tried not to inhale because of the earwax stink. Curled on his side, Jack struggled to drag his left foot in because he didn't want to make Egbert mad. Egbert was Ivor's older brother and he had a loaded pellet pistol.

But there was no room for Jack's left foot. He heard Ivor say, "He doesn't fit."

"We need a saw," stated Egbert.

In the dark of the suitcase, Jack thought of Mr. Skog's saws hanging from nails on the basement wall. There were hacksaws, bow saws, coping saws and even a chainsaw. Through the crack where his foot stuck out, Jack watched Ivor and Egbert's feet. They wore Basket Masters with swastikas on the soles. Jack had swastikas on his shoes, too. They'd all drawn them with pens earlier in the evening and then walked around the basement stamping swastikas on the cement floor.

"We'll get it if we saw his foot off."

Jack heard the fear in Ivor's voice and felt grateful Ivor was trying to help. Jack held his breath and listened for Egbert's response. Egbert circled the suitcase and kicked it as if testing tires.

"It's the suitcase," continued Ivor hopefully. "It's too small."

"It's the biggest one we got." Egbert was four years older than Ivor, and a head taller, and what he said went. Jack heard Egbert crouch down, then felt him grip his foot and with a grunt ram it inside the suitcase. "There." He clapped his hands twice at a job well done. Jack's thighs were now jammed into his breastbone and his forehead was against his knees. Then he felt weight crushing down on him as if he were a bug beneath a board. Egbert was stepping onto the suitcase to force it shut. Jack shouted.

Ivor cried, "Don't!"

Egbert's foot burst through the cardboard and his shoe scraped Jack's cheek. The hot stench of Egbert's sock smothered Jack as if he'd put his face in Mr. Skog's compost box. Egbert tugged his foot free, but his shoe stayed where it was. Jack saw Egbert's eye fill the hole in the suitcase as he peered in, then Egbert's fingers groped Jack's nose as he hunted his shoe and yanked it out.

Steps stomped across the floor upstairs and the door swung open. Mr. Skog shouted down, "*Aag*-baart! *Eev*-aar! What *go*ing's on?"

With Egbert off the suitcase, Jack fought his way out and stood panting and blinking and watching Egbert, who'd shuffled away with his hands in his pockets.

"*Aag*-baart!"

"Nothin'." Shoe in one hand, Egbert frowned and kicked at the floor. Then he added under his breath, but loud enough for Jack and Ivor to hear, "*Dra til helvete!*"

Jack had learned that meant fuck off in Norwegian. Ivor and Egbert were rich sources of information. Ivor said if you pull a hamster's tail its eyes pop out and hang from strings, that an adult human being had fourteen pounds of skin, and that an elephant could fit in a blue whale's mouth.

Mr. Skog muttered and shut the door. Egbert grinned and gave him the finger. It was just the three of them again. Faced with Egbert, there was only one thing Jack could do at that moment and he knew it — laugh. He laughed because cry and you were dead, that was the rule, and Jack would eat dirt rather than look like a sissy. So he kept on laughing, nervously gauging its effect on pig-eyed Egbert who, to his relief, grinned wider, showing his twisted teeth. Egbert was thirteen, red-haired, had warts on his hands and tooth marks on his forearm where his mongoloid sister, Nadia, had bit him.

Jack's dad said Egbert had a one-way ticket to reform school. Jack's dad also said the Skogs' name rhymed with rogue, and a rogue was a crook. Jack had watched the Skogs arrive in the neighbourhood in two separate migrations. First came Mrs. Skog with Nadia and Ivor by train. Then, only four weeks ago, Egbert arrived with Mr. Skog in a pickup truck with a door that had to be tied shut with rope.

Before sticking Jack in the suitcase, Egbert had threatened to make Jack drink wart remover because Egbert wanted to look at Antoine's canaries. Antoine was the old man who lived in the basement suite in Jack's house. He had thirty-six canaries he let fly freely about the room.

"We're gonna look at them canaries," Egbert had said, pressing the Compound W bottle against Jack's mouth.

Jack shook his head and tried not to breathe. He didn't want Egbert near his house, the canaries or Antoine.

"We're gonna look at them birds," said Egbert.

Jack clenched his jaws and shut his eyes.

Egbert pulled his Remington pellet pistol from his back pocket and held it to Jack's temple.

Still Jack refused.

Finally, with Ivor looking on, Egbert gave up on the pistol and the wart remover and forced Jack into the suitcase.

✹

While Jack was in the suitcase, his father and mother, Ray and Lorraine, were drinking rye and seven and watching the news. They were seated on the Danish modern couch, separated by copies of *Chatelaine* and *Life* and a bowl of Liquorice Allsorts.

Ray was watching KVOS, the one U.S. station their rabbit ears picked up. President Johnson announced that the U.S. now had

200,000 ground troops in Vietnam. Ray whistled and shook his head in admiration and said, "Jesus." Various leaders gave their opinions, including Castro, who shook his fist at American imperialism. Ray said, "He's the bastard who killed Kennedy."

Next came a clip showing B-52s gliding in over Vietnamese villages; their crucifix shadows rippling across the huts gave Ray Klein a thrill from his groin to his gullet. He envied the pilots looping in low over those jungles and he recalled his time in Germany in '46 as part of the occupation force. He hadn't expected to like the army, but he'd made friends and felt a part of a magnificent moral cause. The Dutch and the Belgians celebrated the Canadian soldiers because Canadians had liberated them. Men and women wept and shook Ray's hand. It was like being famous, or being the younger brother of someone famous.

Next came the follow-up story on Albert Schell, who was scheduled to leave for Ottawa and then The Hague to stand trial for war crimes.

Ray took the glass bowl of Liquorice Allsorts and occupied himself by picking out the triple-layered ones, peeling them apart, eating the filling then eating the liquorice itself. Sometimes he collected all the triple-layered ones and hid them on Jack and then presented them to him as a gift because Jack loved them, too. It occurred to him that Jack should be in bed soon. He turned to say something to Lorraine but was diverted by the start of *Rat Patrol*. The opening sequence of jeeps cresting a dune made Ray's heart vault. An industrial engineer who'd learned about ordnance in the army, Ray didn't so much watch

Rat Patrol as study it. When the first bout of shooting started he spotted a flaw.

"No way. The eighty-one-millimetre mortar has a maximum range of three thousand yards. For a target like that they'd need a hundred-and-five-millimetre howitzer. Twelve thousand-yard range. Keep your head down, Fritzie boy." He nodded solemnly, recalling the bombed buildings, the cratered streets, the barren-eyed survivors in both France and Germany. He looked at Lorraine, but she was gazing off at the globe in the corner. She was always looking at that globe, in particular at the town of Dieppe, where her father had been killed in the evacuation of 1942. Ray wished he'd been there. In his opinion, occupation troops were nothing more than glorified night watchmen, the clean-up squad, janitors. That was the reason he'd once considered volunteering for Korea.

"Anyway," said Ray, returning to the ongoing subject of the Skogs. "I heard from Rat Gardecki the reason the Skogs moved here is that kid of theirs got booted out of every school in Edmonton. Every school."

"What?"

Ray gestured helplessly. "I'm talking to you."

Lorraine tried hiding her yawn. "Sorry."

Ray hated repeating himself and took it personally when she didn't hear. It was as if she didn't value his opinion. Sometimes he thought she did it on purpose. "The Skogs. Every school. Booted."

"Ivor seems okay."

"Ivor?"

"The youngest. Jack's friend."

"What the hell kind of name is Skog?"

"Norwegian," said Lorraine.

Antoine's canaries began shrieking again downstairs. Ray pointed to the floor and they both listened. "Hear that? Two days now. Doesn't he feed them?" Antoine Gaudin had been living downstairs almost two years, but the birds had never made so much noise. The shrills and cries pierced the floor in steely shrieks that made Ray think of a braking railcar.

⚒

The noise of Antoine's birds made Lorraine think: *les oiseaux, ils se lamentent.* She was always practising her French for the day she finally got to France. She meant to get there with or without Ray, even if she had to take Jack and hitchhike across the country and stow away on a boat.

She'd been thinking about Antoine and France all through the news. Lorraine was barefoot, her legs tucked up under her, wearing a yellow cotton skirt and a white sweatshirt, her sandy blonde hair in a ponytail. Her finger scraped idly at one of her red-painted toenails. She knew Antoine wasn't watching the news because he didn't have a TV. She thought of his soft grey eyes and thick white hair. Ray had a crewcut. Lorraine glanced at him. The muscles in his temples churned as he chewed Liquorice Allsorts. She hated his crewcut. When they had sex his bristly hair pricked her skin; it was like being intimate with a scrub brush. Crewcuts exposed a man's skull, and Ray's was as knuckly as a fist. Jack had a crewcut, but he also had a smooth round head. Of course, hair slicked into a ducktail wasn't any better. The thought of touching hair oiled into place Elvis-style was about as appealing as caressing a greased dog. It occurred to Lorraine that all the pictures depicting Jesus and the angels showed them with long hair; Cyrano de Bergerac had hair to his shoulders and so did the Three Musketeers. Antoine's hair made Lorraine think of a symphony conductor. Antoine was sixty, Ray thirty-nine, Lorraine twenty-four. Ray was lean without being athletic, smoked a pack a day and drank half a dozen cups of coffee. She wished Ray drank more booze, because with a couple of ryes in him he relaxed and became younger and even a little playful. She wished he'd try smoking marijuana; she wished they could both try. Olivia next door said she'd smoked it once. She called it tea, which made it sound tasty. Had Antoine smoked tea? She wondered what Antoine was doing right now.

LBJ's face filled the TV screen. He gazed overtop of his spectacles and announced the number of troops in Vietnam. Lorraine thought Johnson looked like Mr. Magoo. Next came Khrushchev criticizing U.S. meddling. Lorraine thought he looked like a labourer in a slaughterhouse. And there was Canada's Lester Pearson, a constipated banker. Finally, Fidel Castro stood there in army fatigues and beard. Lorraine thought he looked like a poet.

When the story about the Nazi Albert Schell came on, Lorraine shook her head in quiet horror and took note of Ray's reaction. She always watched for his response to things like this because he was Jewish, but more particularly because he pretended not to be Jewish. Ray liked to say he was no more Jewish than John F. Kennedy had been Irish. He was Canadian. *Finito.* He knew no Hebrew or Yiddish, hadn't been bar mitzvahed, had never even set foot in a synagogue and had never opened the Old Testament. He'd point to his fair hair and blue eyes as if they were the final proof. Lorraine's maiden name was Gerard, meaning somewhere back up the line she was French. She wished she could be more French, like from France French, like Antoine. She thought the accent would give her style.

The news ended with a report on the great humanitarian Albert Schweitzer who was in a coma in Gabon, Africa. They showed pictures of Schweitzer as a young man; Lorraine thought he was beautiful. The report described how Schweitzer had given up a brilliant academic career in Germany to establish a hospital in the jungle. Sitting in the living room of their two-bedroom stucco house with its mock mahogany panelling, Lorraine imagined evenings in Africa with the lean and visionary Schweitzer. She imagined the sunsets, the stars, the sounds of the tropical night followed by cock crow, the smell of wood smoke at dawn and drowsy afternoons making love under a mosquito net. Antoine had been to Africa and often talked about Schweitzer. In fact, he was reading his biography. He'd shown it to Lorraine the night before last while Ray was at his ten-year university reunion. She and Antoine had sat on the lawn drinking French wine — *vin rouge* — Cabernet Sauvignon. Lorraine found the wine too tart, but pretended to love it, smiling and rolling it around in her mouth even though it made her teeth feel brittle. Antoine was in an odd and preoccupied mood.

Schweitzer had that effect on him. Or was Antoine beginning to find her tedious? The thought had worried her then and terrified her now. Again she wondered what Antoine was doing.

Two evenings earlier, Antoine Gaudin had opened the cages and the canaries had flapped to the counter and pecked crumbs from the drop-side toaster. They perched on the teepee lamp and on the chairs. A few went to the trickling gooseneck faucet and washed themselves. One beat like a massive moth against the kitchen window trying to escape.

"Okay, okay."

He opened the window and the canary flew off. He raised his hand. "Good luck." Then he shut the window and turned to face the room. Dust and feathers rolled in the tunnel of sunlight illuminating the low-ceilinged suite. Antoine stretched his arms out to the sides and the birds came, in ones and twos, aligning themselves along his arms all the way to his fingers. He wore a short-sleeved white shirt and felt the gentle fishhook pinch of their claws on his skin. For a few moments he stood there like a priest: arms out, face raised, eyes shut, then threw his arms up as if exhorting the faithful to hallelujahs. The canaries scattered.

Gaudin went into the bathroom and took a long time shaving with his bone-handled straight razor. He brushed his collar-length white hair straight back. It amazed him that his forehead was unlined and that his face dared look so serene. He stepped into the bedroom where he'd laid out his black suit along with a pair of shiny black shoes. He put on the suit and shoes and returned to the kitchen with his old clothes rolled in a ball that he pushed into the garbage pail under the sink. He opened the fridge and then the freezer — inhaled the frost-fresh air that reminded him of a certain December outside Krakow — and took out the bottle of Lubelska vodka. He poured an inch into a glass and drank it down. He exhaled hard and his nostrils burned the way they did when he'd worked as a stoker from Gibraltar to Caracas, inhaling the heat hissing from the furnace.

Antoine felt the despair permeating Vancouver as the long weekend signalling the end of summer came to a close. Seasons turning. The evenings already getting shorter, the maple leaves stiffening on the trees and Albert Schweitzer in a coma. The timing was right. Antoine had been waiting for the appropriate moment and this was it. How many hundreds of lives had Schweitzer saved? The man was a saint and could go to his grave with a clear conscience, welcomed to heaven by God and the saints and the angels. Antoine Gaudin imagined Gabon, where Schweitzer had lived, as lush and green and malarial. The only African country he'd visited was Algeria; the land was dry and hard and the locals threw rocks at you.

Canaries careening about his head, Antoine took the vodka to the couch, poured himself another drink, then picked up the envelope on the Formica-topped coffee table and pulled out an old photograph. He gazed at it for a long time. His lips pressed tightly together and a frown creased his forehead. Taking the photo in both hands, he was about to tear it in two but stopped, shut his eyes as if enduring a stab of pain, then opened them. He slipped the photo back into the envelope and wrote *Lorraine* on it. He Scotch-taped the envelope to a beige suitcase and set it by the coffee table.

He felt empty as a bucket, but calm, committed, because everything was finally settled. He looked at the two books on the table, Shakespeare's *Othello* and *Memoirs of Childhood and Youth*, by Schweitzer. Schweitzer's face gazed from the cover: the ascetic saint — far-seeing and forgiving — striding the road of righteousness. Antoine touched the great man's picture as if touching the toes of Christ. On the other cover was Othello, the Moor of Venice, with Iago behind him whispering into his left ear.

Antoine poured more vodka into his glass, set it within reach and then stretched out with his head on a cross-stitched Ukrainian pillow. Reaching into his coat pocket he found a rosary of shiny black beads with an iron crucifix at the end. He kissed the crucifix and thought that even if his lips burned he wouldn't flinch, but press them even tighter to the scorching iron. His high cheekbones lent a Slavic look to his face, his lower lip protruded slightly and his eyes were the colour of gun metal. From his other pocket he took a pill and looked at it: a tooth-sized glass ampoule. For a while he didn't move. Then he sat up and stepped to the window. The sun had dropped behind the house next door so that his room was now in shadow. He opened his fist and looked at the pill lying on the lifeline of his palm. Returning to the couch he reached for the vodka, dropped the pill into his mouth, crushed its glass casing between his molars and at the same time gulped the drink. His hand hit the table and the shot glass rapped the wood, its sharp knock frightening the birds. The last thing he saw was a flurry of wings.

2
Caged Birds

By Tuesday morning Antoine Gaudin's birds were shrilling so loudly they overwhelmed Lorraine's new Beatles record. Ray had to shout to be heard across the breakfast table. He stomped the floor to shut the birds up, but that only caused one of the china cabinet doors to float open.

"Can you at least turn that noise off?"

"It's the Beatles."

"It's eight in the morning."

"I like the Beatles." It was the only thing that diverted her mind from Antoine, whom she hadn't seen since Saturday. She threw down her napkin and went into the living room and switched off the hi-fi. She lifted *A Hard Day's Night* from the platter and slid it back into the paper sleeve. The cover said: *Smart. Irreverent. Electrifying!* Below that were four pictures — nose, eyes and hair — of John, Paul, George and Ringo. In her mind she replayed the opening chord of the title track then the words: *It's been a haaaard daaay's night!*

She returned to the kitchen swinging her hips. When was the last time she and Ray had danced? She said to her son, "Jack likes the Beatles, don't you, Jack?"

Depressed at having to go to school, Jack shrugged and stared at his plate.

Ray said, "He's wrecking the place." It wasn't only the racket coming from the stereo and the birds downstairs that enraged him, but a nose-scalding reek of urine and guano that had been rising from the heat vent.

Lorraine had noticed it too. She didn't want to mention it in case Antoine thought she was complaining. She wanted to tell Ray that Antoine liked the Beatles, but she resisted because it would only anger Ray even more.

Ray saw the music in her hips. "You don't even care."

She shrugged and sat down. As far as Lorraine was concerned Antoine could burn the place to the ground; she'd buy the gas and give him the matches. She shouted over the birds, "You know what I want."

"What about what he wants?" Ray pointed to Jack brooding over his cinnamon toast. "He needs a place to play."

"You don't think they have playgrounds in other places? Or beaches, or mountains or vineyards?"

"*Vineyards*?" Ray let the absurdity of the word hover there between them. He turned to his son. "Hey, Jacko. You want to live in a vineyard?"

Jack tried making himself as small as possible because his parents were yelling. His stomach hurt. He frowned at his cinnamon toast and kept his head down. *Vinyurd?* What was a *vinyurd*? Whenever he was discussed in those tones it meant something bad was going to happen, like a trip to the doctor to get a needle, a trip to the dentist to get his teeth drilled, or the start of school.

"I don't wanna go to school."

"You're going to school," said Ray.

"Everyone goes to school," said Lorraine in a voice filled with false cheer.

Jack knew his mother was pretending. He could tell her sincere voice from her sarcastic voice, both of which were different from her pretending-to-be-excited voice.

Jack's starched shirt and stiff shoes added to his anxiety. Friday he'd had a haircut and the back of his neck still itched. It would take a week for his hair to get comfortable again, even longer for the shoes and shirt to get worked in. His toast was going cold on the grey Melmac plate. The white plastic bag containing Sunbeam bread sat in the middle of the table beside a block of butter. From the side of the bag the yellow-haired Sunbeam Bread girl smiled at him, about to bite into a sagging white slice. Jack and Ivor sometimes packed pieces of that bread into balls and hucked them at crows. On the wall beside the table hung one of his mother's French posters. It showed fruit and wine and dead fish, plus a bird with blood dripping from its mouth. Jack and Ivor had studied that dead bird. His mom said it was a *feznt*. His mom liked French things, which is why she liked Antoine and was always learning French words. He wondered if she would like him more if *he* was French.

"This is a nice house," his dad said as if repeating a lesson. "Sure, it's small, but it's a good little starter house."

Jack heard both pleading and patience in his dad's voice. His parents argued a lot about the house.

Lorraine tapped the rim of her teacup and said nothing.

When they'd moved in, Ray had encouraged Lorraine to decorate any way she wanted, so she covered every wall with French posters including ones of the Eiffel Tower, the Champs Elysées and Versailles. He hadn't said a word about the dead fish and strangled pheasant right here beside the kitchen table staring them in the face when they ate. Now Ray pointed at the lino, a blue crushed marble pattern that matched the Formica table as well as the kitchen counter and the spice tins. "You picked it, remember?" He pointed through the archway to the living room walls. "Mahogany panelling." He pointed to the living room floor. "Solid oak." He pointed to the living room furniture. "Danish Modern. And that TV in there is a Fleetwood."

"Great," said Lorraine. "We can watch *Don Messer's Jubilee.*"

Ray felt betrayed. They'd never watched *Don Messer's Jubilee;* he didn't even like *Don Messer's Jubilee.* He knew what she was up to though; she was needling him about being square, and nothing was squarer than a bunch of middle-aged Maritime fiddlers in string ties. If she thought this would goad him into selling the house, flying off to Europe or South America, or liking the goddamn Beatles, she was wrong. He set his elbow on the table and pointed his finger at her. "Don't try that with me. That's nonsense and you know it."

Lorraine's eyes wavered but held his gaze. She repeated the mantra, *I am not June Cleaver.* If he felt betrayed by her, she felt betrayed by him. What had happened to the affable Ray, the easy-going Ray, the hearty Ray? Where was the Ray who fondly recalled Amsterdam and Liege and Paris? As for decorating, she'd done it for him, for his colleagues, for the neighbours, to demonstrate that she could, just as she used to dress for him, doing her best to look and think the way she thought he wanted her to. No more. This morning she'd committed the quiet insubordination of throwing on the same sweatshirt and yellow cotton skirt she'd worn last night. Her hair, as usual, was pulled back in a ponytail. The only concession to style was the touch of mascara that accented the length of her eyes, giving them a hint of the Mediterranean. There would be no bubble curls, flips or beehives for her. Once Ray was out of the house, though, she'd change into something tight and pop in on Antoine. She had coffee with him every morning. Talking to Antoine was like opening the windows, like checking her horoscope, and this morning she was more anxious than ever to see to him.

Ray turned to his son. "Hey, Jacko. Isn't this a great house?"

Jack shrank turtle-like into the collar of his stiff new shirt. His dad sat to his right and his mother to his left. He could feel them both watching him and could tell his dad wanted him to say yes. His dad's breath smelled of coffee, his skin of cologne, and he had Kleenex stuck to his neck where he'd cut himself shaving. His dad made faces at himself in the mirror as he shaved and the razor made a crackly sound as it scraped his skin. If his dad was in a good mood he'd give Jack whisker rubs before he shaved. They hurt, but Jack liked them.

Each Saturday morning Jack and his dad sat on the couch and watched *All-Star Wrestling* on channel 8. There was Haystack Calhoun, a huge fat farmer with shoulder-length hair who wrestled in overalls and wore a horseshoe around his neck for good luck. There was Don Leo Jonathon, Gene Kiniski and Eric Froelich who wrestled barefoot. There was also Sweet Daddy Siki, who had curly white hair and entered the ring carrying a perfume bottle and sprayed his opponents so they didn't stink. When *All-Star Wrestling* was over, Jack and his dad practised the moves: the half nelson, the full nelson, the hammerlock and the sleeper. That was the best time of the week. Weekday mornings were the worst because his parents argued.

Jack hadn't said a word about Egbert Skog sticking him in the suitcase, because he knew if he finked his dad would go after Egbert and maybe put the sleeper on him and when Egbert woke up he'd sneak into their house, open the drawer and spit in his dad's underpants.

"Isn't this a great house?" his dad repeated.

Jack had no idea if this was a great house, though he knew a lot about it. He knew the clatter of a pebble dropped through the heat vent rattling along the sheet metal duct. He liked to stand by the heat vent when the furnace clicked on and blew air up inside his pant legs inflating them. He knew the clean smell of the linen closet. He knew there were numbers stamped on the underside of the kitchen chairs and that the electrical outlets looked like two shocked faces one above the other.

But Jack was more interested in the world outside. The carport had jam jars full of rusty screws, stacked wood and a bench with a vice you could crush things in. The yard had the plum tree and the alley had garbage cans that were treasure chests of discarded bottles and radios. There was the pipe that ran under the road that he and Ivor crawled through to reach enemy lines. Ivor Skog's house used to be Miss Funt's house. Jack had heard his mom say Miss Funt lived on digestive biscuits and Darjeeling tea, and when she died the police discovered hundreds of tea and biscuit boxes stacked in the basement. Now Miss Funt's house was the Skogs' house and it had mice. They ran along the floor by the walls while Egbert shot at them with his pellet pistol. Jack wished their house had mice. He looked up at his father. "Ivor's got mice!"

"See." Ray turned to Lorraine as if his point had been made.

Lorraine said nothing. When she thought of their East Van neighbourhood she saw row after row of stucco boxes occupied by men with ducktails or crewcuts and women with back-combed hair. When she and Ray first moved in, Olivia Edson next door had been a source of strength. They shared disdain for the bleak backwater of Vancouver, but despite all her talk, fifty-three-year-old Olivia had let herself get stuck here. She'd had all manner of opportunities to leave — or so she said — talking wistfully about the men who'd fallen in love with her and wanted to take her away. Olivia's papery cheeks and creased forehead made Lorraine think of an aging actress who'd spent too much time drunk in the sun. From day one, Olivia Edson had taken it upon herself to mentor Lorraine, advising her on everything from stain removal to male psychology to the Pill. Olivia still talked of being an actress, even though she worked afternoons as a cashier in a Rexall and went out with Rat Gardecki, who ran the gas station at the corner. It was Olivia who'd told her all about Miss Funt and the other neighbours.

Doreen Funt? Wing nut. Walks around that backyard cutting slugs in two with a butcher knife. Has every record Mario Lanza ever made.

The gimp on the other side of you? That's Gene Rosencko. Born that way. Still lives with his mother. Seen her yet? God. Figure like a fridge. You must've got a whiff of the cabbage by now. They both put garlic in their shoes.

Dolly Gooch? Widow's pension. Bingo five days a week. Has a crush on Jack LaLane. Says she went to school with Raymond Burr.

When Miss Funt died and the Skogs moved in, Lorraine got to know Eva Skog because Jack chummed with Ivor, but generally Lorraine kept to herself. This side of Vancouver or that, it was all the same to her: trees and rain, rain and trees. They weren't tropical or exotic trees, just gloomy cedars and firs, and the rain was not warm, but cold and depressing. Vancouver was a grim, dark bush on the edge of the chill, damp world, and every year it got harder to bear. The only thing she liked about Vancouver was the port, because ships meant travel and travel meant getting away — to San Francisco, to South America, to Europe.

As an act of rebellion she'd recently let the hair on her legs and under her arms sprout. Ray said she looked like something out of *National Geographic*. When she'd told him how Antoine said French women never shaved their armpits, Ray had been livid. He'd shouted that Antoine better keep his nose out of her armpits. Lorraine had to talk fast to keep Ray from going downstairs and booting Antoine out right then and there. She couldn't bear the thought of Antoine leaving.

Now Ray stood up from the table. He didn't want to argue, he hated arguing. All he wanted was to once, just once, head off to work whistling. It was eight in the morning and here he was already sweating. And the damn birds were giving him a headache. "Stinks like rotten eggs," he said. "What's the guy doing down there?"

Lorraine tried to appear bored. She leaned her head on her left hand and with her right turned her teacup side to side on the saucer. "He's got a few canaries," she said for the hundredth time. But she was wondering, too. The birds didn't usually stink and they rarely made such a racket.

Ray watched her. Her nails were chewed and the polish chipped. Her eyebrows were darker than her hair, which made an attractive contrast. She was a good-looking woman, a beautiful woman, and when she smiled — rarely, lately — he thought her teeth were as perfect as Chiclets. "A sixty-year-old man in a basement suite full of canaries," he said.

Lorraine continued to turn her teacup left then right. She hated Ray talking about Antoine. Ray's remarks were like grubby fingerprints. "So?"

"So I'd say that's a bit weird." When Lorraine didn't respond Ray got bolder. He placed both hands flat on the table and leaned toward her. "Who is he? Some Frog who shows up out of nowhere, bargains you down on the rent —"

Lorraine looked up. "He did not! And he's not a Frog."

"Sure he is."

"Are you a kike?"

Ray shot her a silent *shut up!* He glanced at Jack, who was frowning at his plate. "What's he doing telling you to stop shaving your armpits?"

At that, Lorraine sat back and laughed.

"Sure. Go ahead."

"Grow a moustache," said Lorraine.

"I don't like moustaches."

"I do."

"Then you grow one. You're growing everything else." Ray watched her cross her arms and knew he'd insulted her. Her grey eyes turned as cold as ball bearings. Her crossed arms accentuated her breasts. Besides thinking it would be good for her, one of the reasons he wanted her to get pregnant again was it'd make her breasts bigger. He liked the look of them in a tight sweater.

Lorraine said, "God, that's an ugly tie." He wore a white short-sleeved button-down shirt with a plastic pocket liner full of mechanical pencils and shiny pens.

"Yeah? You bought it for me."

"No, you *told* me to buy it for you."

Ray shouted, "Right! I'm an ogre. Thanks a helluva lot!"

Lorraine yelled back, "Well, if you want to look like a middle-aged drone-of-an-insurance-salesman, go ahead!"

"Whataya expect? Beatle boots? Blue suede shoes?"

"How the hell —"

They caught themselves. They looked at Jack stabbing his toast with his fork.

Jack looked up at the sudden quiet. His parents were watching him. He felt tears ooze from his eyes the way the blood oozed from the *feznt's* mouth. He imagined his dad with a moustache and his mother in France. France was in *Yerup* and *Yerup* was on the globe in the corner of the living room. His parents looked as if they expected him to say something.

"Ivor's dad's got a beard."

"That's not all he's got," said Ray.

Lorraine watched Ray shake his head and go to the sink and rinse his hands. Saturday night, after sex, Ray had put his hands behind his head, gazed up at the ceiling as if at the constellations, and told her gears were elegance in iron. He began telling her about herringbone gears, epicyclic gears, crossed-axis helical gears. He actually got up and wheeled Jack's bicycle into the bedroom to demonstrate the concept of torque. Lorraine missed the concept because she watched Ray more than the demonstration itself, touched by such ingenuous enthusiasm yet wondering how she'd married such a creature. Had her father been like that? Antoine certainly wasn't. Ray was her first and only lover and sex was not what she'd expected, certainly nothing like in novels or movies. They made love like a couple dancing in shoes that pinched. And though Ray was always gentle, Lorraine found sex more frustrating than pleasurable, as if, like awkward dancers, neither knew how to lead or where to place their feet. Saturday night he'd been particularly gentle and that made her feel guilty and sad, especially thinking of Antoine just downstairs, so near. Perhaps he even overheard. Why did Antoine have to be thirty-six years older than she was? Why couldn't she have met him on some country road in Provence next to a vineyard or a field of lavender? Despite his time in Europe with the army, Ray had no interest in Provence or Paris or vineyards ripening in the southern sun.

"The real way to win a war," Ray had told her after putting Jack's bicycle away, "is not to kill the enemy, but to wipe out their ball-bearing plants. No ball bearings, no war machine. *Finito.*" "That," Ray had said, "was why the Allies threw so much weight against the Schweinfurt ball bearing factory." Apparently Ray considered this something Lorraine should know. Lying there on the cooling sheets in the moonlit room, Lorraine had kept herself a continent away by picturing that field of lavender.

And yet even though Lorraine was elsewhere she had to admit that at one time — seven years ago — everything about Ray had aroused and intrigued her. There was his solidity, for one thing; he was like a statue on a granite plinth. There was his male paraphernalia: his keys on their flywheel key chain, his expansion bracelet Rolex, his U.B.C. Engineers ring, his U.B.C. Engineers lighter, his Rothmans, his Wilkinson Sword razor, his Spanish leather wallet, the pennies in his penny loafers. These things had been, for her, the ritual objects of a sultan, mysterious and golden and imbued with power. And it had rubbed off on her, because when she'd started going out with Ray she was transformed from a teenager into an adult. Ray drove, had a degree, had been to France, had a career. He knew where he was going and how to get there. He knew about transverse axles, pneumatic drills, metal fatigue; it all made sense to him. He understood hydraulics, something that to Lorraine was nothing more than a set of strange sounds: *high – draw – licks.* And there was his Jewishness. To Lorraine, being Jewish meant being part of rituals ancient and awesome, and she wanted that; she believed she needed it. She was crushed to discover he was an atheist. Ray summed up his attitude toward religion in one word: "Bunk."

That had been their first argument.

"But Ray, Judaism —"

"Judaism!" The look he gave her was a slammed door. He'd looked at her as if she was some dizzy Arts major waxing on about the importance of Wordsworth to Western Civilization. To Ray, Jew meant victim. It meant being outside. It meant alienation. Who the hell needed that? Life was tough enough. He'd spent his life trying to get on and fit in. Even if he wanted to seek out his roots there was hardly a Jewish community in Vancouver to speak of. "You want me to grow a beard and —"

He waved his hands about his ears meaning sidelocks. "You want to move to Israel and live on a kibbutz and dig irrigation ditches?"

"Ray —"

"And you want to shave your head?"

"Ray —"

"You want to put a board down the middle of our bed when you're on your monthly?"

"Ray —"

"Bunk! All religion is bunk! Religion is the reason there are wars!"

Lorraine had shouted back, "Then why did you go overseas? Why did you join the army? Wasn't it because of Hitler? Wasn't it to liberate your people?"

He'd gazed at her in silence, impressed once again by her intensity but frustrated by her naïveté. He spoke quietly, with calm. "Why? Because I had nowhere else to go. Because everyone else in my family was dead." Then he'd added, "And what do you mean — my people? You're my people. You."

That had touched her. That had made her want to cry.

So she had accepted there would be no conversion to Judaism, no Jewish wedding. She had accepted that ham with applesauce was Ray's favourite dinner, and bacon and eggs his breakfast of choice. When Jack was born there was no ritual; he wasn't even baptized. As for the circumcision, there was no bris and the procedure was not performed by a *mohel* but by a general practitioner named Harrigan who did it for no other reason than hygiene.

✄

Lorraine reached across the kitchen table and placed her hand reassuringly on Jack's shoulder. "Eat your breakfast."

His cinnamon toast — a first-day-of-school treat — lay mangled on his plate.

"I don't wanna go to school." He said it quietly, so his dad wouldn't get angry and say he was whining, and his mother wouldn't get frustrated and withdraw and stare at the globe.

"School's fun," lied Lorraine, remembering the confinement and the tedium.

"Sure," said Ray. "You'll learn things."

"I don't wanna learn things."

Jack had seen his classroom and met his teacher on Friday and he didn't like either of them. The room smelled of paint and floor wax and the desks were cold. School was going to be worse than kindergarten. His Grade One teacher had the same slicked back hair and widow's peak as Count Dracula.

"Of course you want to learn things," said Ray. "You don't learn things you'll end up being a garbage man."

"Oh, God," said Lorraine, seeing what was coming.

"But I wanna be a garbage man," said Jack, suddenly enthusiastic.

Ray considered his son, then looked at Lorraine. "That's your doing."

Lorraine batted her eyelids and crooned with sweet sarcasm, "Don't be late for work, dear."

Ray didn't have the energy to respond. He lifted his blazer from the back of the chair, gave it a brush with the back of his hand and draped it over his forearm. The blazer bore the gold crest of the University of British Columbia Engineers. Out of habit he recited to himself: *We're the engineers! We can drink forty beers!* His calfskin briefcase waited in its spot on the tube-metal-and-vinyl chair by the door. When he picked it up he felt its reassuring heft. Jack's Aladdin's lamp lunch box was on the chair as well. Ray reached for the doorknob. On the door hung a four-foot long and two-foot wide Selwyn Industrial Engineering Ltd. calendar for the year 1965. The previous month's page had featured a girl in a bathing suit beside an internal gear and pinion. This month's page featured a full-colour picture of a red-haired woman in a red bikini posing beside a bench on which a series of worm and gear pairs were arranged in increasing size.

Lorraine hated the calendar, but Ray insisted it was the only calendar big enough for his notes. Ray filled the square for each day with reminders and appointments and made sure to consult it on his way out the door each morning. But on this particular morning, Ray was about to leave without giving it a glance.

"Ray."

He turned.

"Don't forget to check your horoscope." She pointed to the calendar.

Ray gave her the hard eye but was too meticulous a man not to look at the note he'd left himself. When he'd read it he put the heel of his hand to his forehead as if to push the contents of his frontal lobe back into place. There it was in the square for September 7th in his own neat script, *Jack. 1st day school.* How could he forget? They'd just talked about it.

"What do you expect with all that?" He pointed to the floor and the racket downstairs. He saw Lorraine was watching him and so was Jacko. Seeking some sort of gift to mark the momentous day, Ray patted his pockets and found, among his pens, the gold one he'd pinched from Charlene's desk at the office, a sleek little number that was too thin for him anyway, and, with all the verve with which one can wield a swiped pen, he presented it to his son as a first-day-of-school memento. "There you go, Jacko."

Jack frowned at the pen lying there beside his plate of mashed cinnamon toast. He didn't want a pen, he wanted a cutlass, and if he couldn't get a cutlass he wanted smothering gloves, the black leather kind worn by assassins on *The Man from U.N.C.L.E.* He'd asked for smothering gloves last Christmas, but all he got was mittens.

Ray watched Jack; no doubt about it, the boy was his mother's son. Ray wanted Jack to take the pen apart and marvel at its inner workings, to appreciate the miracle of spring and pin, to be intrigued by how things did what they did, but so far the boy demonstrated no inclination to do anything other than collect pop bottles. It took him ages to grasp the concept of brakes on his bicycle, so long in fact that he developed the habit of running the bike into the nearest hedge to stop. And then there was the kid's habit of wandering off. Three times Ray had discovered him — by fluke — miles from home, toodling along like a hobo. One of those times Ray had had

Charlene in the car. He'd had to get rid of her *tout de suite*, which pissed her off, especially since they'd been on the way to her place for a poke. He'd given her cab fare and left her on a corner. When he'd got Jack home he'd given Lorraine holy hell for letting the boy wander around like that. This had the added benefit of directing attention away from what Ray was doing driving around in the middle of the day.

Ray took out one of his mechanical pencils, bent to the calendar and added to the square for September 7, 1965: *Jack. Pen. Demo. 7:00 – 7:30.* Pocketing his mechanical pencil, Ray winced again at the stink rising from the vent in the floor and looked at Lorraine as if to say it was her fault, which of course it was, given that she was the one who'd let the guy move in. Between the stench and the noise his head was pounding. Today of all days he didn't need a headache, because today he was seeing Charlene, his piece of cake, his bit on the side. Charlene, stacked and sultry, could model for the Selwyn Engineering calendar.

✄

Leaving Jack to finish his breakfast, Lorraine followed Ray out to the carport. He wasn't jingling his keys in his pocket as he walked. Ray always jingled his keys as he walked, so Lorraïne assumed he was obsessing over Antoine and his birds. "Don't worry. I'll talk to him."

They reached the Thunderbird. "Maybe we should up the rent."

"I said, I'll talk to him."

"We should up the rent anyway. I mean —" Ray gestured toward the basement suite as if to say look what we have to put up with. The birds were still shrieking, a loud metallic ringing like something from a factory. "Place's gonna need fumigating. And *he's* getting the bill."

Ray got in the car and closed the door. It shut with a solid sound, a thick chunk of a sound that he called "the sweet sound of quality engineering." Lorraine watched the electric window whirr down and Ray slide the steering wheel over. That always struck her as unnatural and dangerous. Ray said it locked when you released the footbrake, yet to Lorraine it was a frightening reliance on technology. What happened if the steering wheel started doing that when you were driving? Ray said that was impossible. She didn't believe it, which frustrated him. Everything frustrated him these days. He slid the key into the ignition with an almost sensuous touch that made Lorraine envious.

"I want to drive," she said.

"Drive what, nails?"

Lorraine didn't bother responding.

"Fine," said Ray. "Get your licence."

"Okay."

"But you're not touching the Bird."

"Why?"

"Why, why, why. You sound like Jack." He started the car, causing a great rumble of sound to gurgle up around them. "Listen to that. It's a V8."

"So?"

"So that's why you can't drive this car. You don't appreciate it." He could just imagine her with the Bird; she'd end up in San Francisco smoking Mary Jane with the hippies.

"You're trying to control me."

Ray frowned at her hips. "You wore those clothes last night. What happened to the pedal-pushers I bought you?"

"Well, it's a trade-off, Ray. Be able to breathe or wear pants two sizes too small."

"They were a present!"

"They gave me cramps!" She told him not to buy her clothes but he went ahead and did it anyway — always too small and always too tight — as if she were a kid, as if she didn't know how to dress herself. He'd started doing it just after they were married. At first she liked the idea because it made her feel taken care of. Then she saw where it was all headed: he was turning her into Doris Day. It took two years for her to get up the nerve to tell him. He was hurt.

Now, eyes gleaming with hope, Ray studied her stomach. "Are you — ?"

"No."

"You're not on the Pill?" he said warningly.

"No."

"The Pill causes cancer."

"I'm not on the Pill."

"You want cancer? *The Big C?*"

She crossed her arms and stared up at the carport rafters.

"It got Bogie. Bogie died of cancer."

"Humphrey Bogart was on the Pill?"

"Don't be an asshole."

With the Thunderbird warmed up, Ray hit the gas pedal, dropped the idle, then thrust his chin toward Antoine's suite. "Well, something's going on down there. Sounds like that movie, *The Birds.*"

Lorraine didn't think that at all. She imagined a French village at sunset with people seated at outdoor cafés and the birds chirping in the trees.

Ray released the emergency brake, locking the steering wheel, and then put the car in reverse and backed out, white-wall tires crunching softly over the gravel.

When Ray was gone Lorraine headed for Antoine's door. She hadn't seen Antoine since Saturday night when she'd told him how she felt about him. He hadn't responded as she'd hoped. Sunday and Monday she'd avoided him out of anger and humiliation. Was she not attractive enough? Was she too young? Too provincial? The birds gave her an excuse to talk to him, though she'd have to be careful not to complain. She practised her opening line: *I was just wondering if the birds were okay ...*

On her way to see him she remembered Jack still in the kitchen. She shouted from the yard, "Jack. Jack, get ready for school. I'll be up in a minute."

3
Strangers

The birds shrilled so loudly — a rhythmic REE! REE! — that Lorraine had to pound the door. When Antoine didn't answer, she stepped to the left and looked in the window. Canaries beat against the glass, winged about the room, perched on the counter, the table and on the couch where Antoine lay stretched out in a suit.

"Antoine ... Antoine!" She rapped the window, diamond ring clicking the glass. He looked frozen, one leg jackknifed, his mouth raked wide.

Taking the stairs three at a time she grabbed the extra key from its nail in the kitchen. When she opened Antoine's door a gush of birds drove her away.

Jack, who'd followed her hoping that whatever was going on was serious enough to get him out of going to school, watched the birds flee screaming to the plum tree. "They're getting away!" He leapt about trying to catch them.

Arm shielding her face, Lorraine stepped into the room. When the birds were gone she lowered her arm. Her stomach heaved. Antoine's face was glazed in guano and his eyes pecked to jelly. "Oh God ..." She stumbled out and leaned against the plum tree and retched.

"Mom?"

She looked up. Jack had climbed the tree after the birds and was gazing down at her, fear bewildering his eyes. She said nothing, just wiped her mouth, turned, and, palm cupped over her nose against the low-creeping smell, plunged back in and opened the room's one window. She found Jack next to her, gazing round-eyed at Antoine.

"Out! Now!" She hustled him out the door. "Upstairs!" She clapped her hands. "Go on! Move!" When he was gone, Lorraine re-entered the basement suite and spotted the suitcase, the one she'd lent him just a few weeks back for the trip he'd said he was taking. Taped to it was a white envelope with her name on it. Knees buckling, she lost her balance and leaned on the table. She didn't want to see Antoine like this.

She whispered, "Antoine ..." He remained rigid, mouth stretched, lips shrunken, and his eyes ... She reached for his wrist to test his pulse, but his hand was an upturned claw. She withdrew her fingers and held them against herself. In the distance she heard a siren and listened until the sound faded.

She turned slowly, as if in a trance, and walked upstairs to call the police.

She found Jack in the middle of the kitchen with his knuckles in his mouth. She hugged him, warding off the gruesome images she imagined beating like bats about his brain.

"It's okay. It's okay." She put him down, then stroked his crewcut head.

Jack gazed at her.

"Put your shoes on."

"They're on."

"Where's your lunch box and school bag?"

He pointed to the door.

"Okay, okay." Her ponytail had come undone. She brushed her hair back.

"What happened to Antoine's eyes?"

Lorraine forced herself to speak soothingly. "He's sick." She saw that wasn't enough. "You've been sick. Remember?"

"Has he got mumps?"

"No. He hasn't got mumps."

"Is he going to die?"

She heard wonder and fear and thrill in Jack's voice. "We'll talk about it later. Now get going." She watched him follow the trail of cement slabs inset into the grass leading to the carport and the alley. She'd meant to walk him to school, but the idea of leaving Antoine lying there dead in the basement appalled her. Besides, the school was only three blocks away and Jack played there all the time. She reached for the phone and dialled zero. When the operator came on Lorraine's throat turned dry as rope.

The operator said, "Hello?"

"Police, please." While she waited, she wound her finger in the cord until it turned the same colour as Antoine's face. She shook her hand free. She heard female voices from the party line twittering in the background. It was as if they were in her own head. She thought of her mother's voices and hallucinations. The people on the party line were too faint to make out, but the tone suggested $1.49 Day at Woodward's and soap operas. "Shut up!" Lorraine cupped her hands around the receiver. "Shut up!" The voices hesitated, like birds at the sound of a slammed door, then resumed. Eventually she got the police. She shut her eyes, "I want to report a —" she balked at the word suicide, " — a death."

When she hung up, Lorraine looked around the kitchen: the remains of breakfast, the still life with pheasant, Ray's calendar. The fridge motor clicked off and the silence was sickening. She thought of Antoine down there, dead, amid that smell, and she began to tremble. Not knowing what else to do, she watched herself go onto the porch and down the stairs. As she approached the basement door it seemed to slide toward her like a mouth opening wide.

A suit. Antoine had put on a suit. What else could it be but suicide? His face was the colour of lard and for the first time she noticed that his fingertips were blue-black. His hands were always so precise in their gestures and now they looked frostbitten. He'd destroyed himself and abandoned her. Of all her churning emotions the uppermost was insult. She was feeling insulted.

She picked up the heavy suitcase then set it back down and glanced at Antoine. Her stomach slithered like guts on a butcher's slab, and she saw Cosgrove's marble countertop askew with pink and purple intestines. She hurriedly took the suitcase upstairs to the living room closet. When she opened the door something shifted, something big — her heart jerked in her chest. *Jack!* Hiding in the closet between the coats. She hauled him out. "I told you to go to school!"

"What about his birds?"

"They'll be fine."

"They flew away!"

"They're birds, Jack, birds."

"Is Antoine better?"

"Come on."

They didn't walk to school, they ran: down the alley, across 20th, down the next alley and across 19th. The schoolyard was empty. Many times Jack had told Lorraine that the old brick school building looked like Riverview Mental Hospital where his grandma Estelle lived, where he'd seen an old lady tied to a bed like the lady in the cartoon tied to the railroad tracks.

Lorraine and Jack stood at the chain-link fence enclosing the schoolyard. "You know the way."

He began biting his nails.

Lorraine pulled his fingers from his mouth. "We were there Friday. Room 102. In the door and down the stairs."

"Are you gonna use bread?"

She looked at him, fearful, curious. "What are you talking about?"

"For the birds."

Lorraine took his hand and together they ran across the schoolyard. Jack began to laugh. Lorraine recalled running with him across the hard sand at the beach. She remembered the smell of Coppertone, of eating fish and chips with salt and vinegar. Jack had collected pop bottles and built sandcastles with Ray, intricate sandcastles with tunnels and towers and moats, and they'd battled the sea when the tide came in. She thought of the day they went to the beach on a bright blue winter afternoon, just her and Jack, when no one else was around, and it was as if the beach was theirs. Jack had never been to the beach in winter. They watched the waves smash the shore and the water fizz across the sand, Lorraine's hair blowing sideways in the wind.

They reached the foot of the school steps. "Room 102," said Lorraine. "In the door and down the stairs. We were there Friday. You saw your room and met your teacher. Remember?"

Jack shook his head.

Lorraine was losing her patience. "Yes, Jack, you do remember." With her finger she wrote 102 in the dirt. "Room 102."

"I don't wanna go to school."

"No one wants to go to school, but that's the way it is." She heard how hard that sounded, but left it at that and prodded him up the steps. During the orientation Friday, she'd seen the look in his eyes at the sight of his teacher, Glen Gough. Gough was too tall, his suit too dark, his smile too wide. Lorraine didn't like Gough either, especially when he began outlining his Sink or Swim method of education. She decided men shouldn't teach Grade One. When Jack reached the top of the steps he turned to her.

"Can I have them?"

"Have what?"

"The birds."

Watching her son sometimes made Lorraine believe in reincarnation. She wondered if she'd been chosen to escort him into this his next life, a life that had little to do with her or with Ray. He resembled her physically, yes, but from the start he'd had his own whimsical logic, finding it perfectly reasonable to keep a mannequin's hand — rooted from a garbage can — under his bed, to Scotch-tape his sweater to his bedroom wall to keep the room warm, to ask for a ladder so he could climb up and pick clouds. *Mon fils, il est un étranger.*

When Lorraine got back home there were two cops waiting on the lawn, an older one with a flattened nose fanning himself with his notepad and the other one wiping bird droppings from his shoulder. At the curb, the police car's red light spun round and round on the roof.

"Ma'am. You were —"

Lorraine nodded numbly. She opened Antoine's door — it would always be Antoine's door — and they all stepped into the basement suite together, like a delegation. Without getting too close, the two cops looked Antoine over, taking him in from all angles but not touching him, as if they feared he might be wired to explosives. Lorraine looked around. Apart from the feathers and guano and scattered seed that crunched under-foot, the basement suite was clean, the dishes done, the LPs slotted neatly in their wire rack, the lid closed on the record player. The walls were blank but for the poster of the domes of Sacré-Coeur in Montmartre, which Lorraine had hung before Antoine moved in. He'd done no decorating and brought no furniture. He hadn't lived in this suite so much as occupied it.

Aside from the birds, the one sign of his presence was the stack of newspapers by the door. Antoine was a great reader of newspapers, and not just the *Province* and *Columbian*, but the *Globe and Mail*, and, every Sunday, the *New York Times*. She'd noticed how he scanned the papers as if hunting some particular bit of information. When the kids came around on paper drives, Antoine Gaudin had the biggest bundle on the block, something Lorraine knew made Jack proud. The neat-ness of the room emphasized to her how thoroughly Antoine had planned this.

The older cop was about fifty and so tall his head almost brushed the ceiling. "This the way you found him?"

"Yes."

"You touch anything?"

Without thinking, Lorraine said, "No."

Two books sat on the coffee table. The older cop picked one up and turned it over suspiciously. "Albert Schweitzer," he said. "Didn't he just die?"

Lorraine nodded.

The cop grunted, replaced the book on the table and, exhal-ing, turned to the grim business of the corpse. His young partner stood back, deferring to the older man who, cringing slightly, stepped closer and leaned to give Antoine's face a sniff. "Almonds."

The younger cop said, "Maybe he choked on them?"

The older cop exhaled hard and gave him a fatigued look. Then he reached inside Antoine's coat pocket and found a wallet.

The younger cop said, "Light's better outside."

No one argued. The smell was not just almonds but other things, things Lorraine didn't want to imagine. They all stepped outside. Unlike Ray's wallet, Antoine's was thin. The cop went through it with his big fingers. He was a nail-biter and smelled of leather. Lorraine looked up at his broken nose and his scrubbed skin, and watched his thick fingers struggle to tweeze a card from a slot. When he got it out, he read it at arm's length.

"Antoine Gah-din."

"Go-dan."

The cop looked at Lorraine.

"He's French," she said.

"Canadian?"

"Excuse me?"

"French Canadian?" asked the cop. "A Canadian citizen?"

"No. From France. Or, I don't know. Maybe he's a citizen ..." Lorraine had never asked. She'd assumed — but what had she assumed?

He found a snapshot in Antoine's wallet and studied it. His gaze shifted from the picture to Lorraine to the picture. "You were close?"

She loved him. That's what she had told Antoine Saturday night: she loved him. That's when things went sour, that's when Antoine withdrew. Now she didn't want to love him. She was abandoned and insulted and about to fall apart. She shrugged weakly.

The cop turned the picture so Lorraine could see it. *Her.*

PART TWO

THE DAY UNFOLDS

4

A New Life

Jack watched Mr. Gough pace the front of the classroom slapping his palm with a yardstick. Jack's dad had never even spanked him, much less hit him with a yardstick, though Jack had seen Mr. Skog clout Egbert with his boot. Mr. Skog had been sitting on the back steps polishing the boot and said, "Look," and when Egbert looked, Mr. Skog whacked him and said, "There," as if Egbert had it coming.

Mr. Gough's suit was so dark and shiny it looked like it was made of black plastic. Jack thought of a commandant. There were commandants in *The Great Escape*, commandants who shot people and shoved them in ditches. Jack's dad had taken him and his mom to the Coronet Theatre downtown to see *The*

Great Escape. Steve McQueen wore a leather jacket and jumped a motorcycle over a barbed wire fence. Jack wished he had a leather jacket instead of new brown corduroys, a new white shirt and new brown shoes from the Army & Navy. The shoes felt like boxes, the corduroys smelled like dog fur and the shirt felt like the shower curtain. They'd also bought a Hilroy notebook that smelled of bleach, two HB pencils that smelled of wood, a pencil sharpener, a wooden ruler with a metal edge and a Pink Pearl eraser. The eraser had a rubbery taste and rubbery feel between Jack's molars when he chewed it. These were his school supplies and school was where his mother said he had to go every weekday from nine to three. Jack had repeated that to himself: 9, 2, 3, and felt the same panic he did whenever his mother announced he had to go to the dentist.

"There are two kinds of letters," said Mr. Gough, pacing the front of the room. "Who can tell me what those two kinds might be?" When no one spoke, Mr. Gough ceased pacing but continued slapping his palm with his stick and scanning the class. Jack watched in panic as Gough's gaze settled, as he knew it would, on him. Mr. Gough had oily skin like Egbert Skog and he'd told them his name — Gough — rhymed with tough.

"Jack," he said, reading the name card Jack had so carefully written out in black crayon. The way Mr. Gough said his name made it sound strange, like it wasn't a name at all, but a sound — whack! — like the sound of an axe splitting wood. "Jack. What are the two kinds of letters?"

Jack didn't need to look around to know everyone was watching him. He could feel it: like bugs crawling down his neck.

"Well, Jack?"

Jack didn't know. No one told him he'd have to know things. He felt like an empty box. An empty box was hollow and hollow was a windy-sounding word with nothing in it. Jack tried to think about Mr. Gough's question, but all he could think of was his stiff shoes and plastic shirt and grey desk. He could sense Ivor in the next row keeping his head down. Ivor had warned him to sit at the back and keep his head low or the teacher would ask him questions. Ivor had gone through Grade One twice so he knew all about it. Jack repeated the question to himself: What are the two kinds of letters? He concentrated. The mailman brought letters and put them through the letter slot in their front door. The mailman wore a hat and carried a sack and sometimes talked to the milkman who'd run over Olivia Edson's poodle. For weeks there'd been a bloodstain on the road with bits of fur in it.

"Speak up."

Jack opened his mouth and for a moment thought he would be sick, the way he'd been sick when he drank the jar of pickle juice. But instead of being sick, words flew from his mouth like the canaries flying from Antoine's cages. "Boy and girl!"

Mr. Gough's black eyebrows jumped up, wrinkling his forehead. Then they settled back down and Mr. Gough stared hard at Jack as if he couldn't see him very well, as if he wasn't sure who Jack was.

Jack waited like a bug on the floor.

"Jack says there are boy letters and there are girl letters."

From somewhere came a titter. Jack's mother had taught

him the alphabet, but his answer had nothing to do with her tutoring, it came from the same strange source that told him cats were female dogs.

"Tell us, Jack. Can you give us examples of boy letters and girl letters?"

Jack couldn't.

Mr. Gough opened his mouth and laughed loudly. Everyone relaxed because Mr. Gough was happy. Jack breathed more easily. It was good when the teacher was happy, especially when the teacher was a man, because according to Ivor Skog man teachers were mean. Ivor said he had a man teacher who beat him with a shaving strap.

Mr. Gough continued to laugh, then suddenly slammed the desk with his yardstick. "No!"

Jack flinched. Everyone else looked scared now, too. Jack knew three others in the room, Ivor, Fat Boy Burton and Miriam. Ivor had told Jack only last week that he and Egbert had tied Fat Boy Burton to a tree and put a dead seagull on his head. Jack knew Miriam lived two blocks over and had raspberry bushes. He doubted Miriam knew what the two types of letters were even though he'd seen her Saturday mornings at the library reading books without pictures.

"This is a big question. A fifty-cent question. There are two types of letters: vowels and consonants. Vowels are soft; consonants are hard. Repeat."

They repeated.

"Again!"

They repeated it again and Jack heard the fearful voices

vibrating around him like birds.

"These are the vowels: *a, e, i, o, u*, and sometimes *y*. Now," continued Mr. Gough, "some letters live alone. Other letters live in families. The letter 'I' for example. 'I' lives alone. Whereas *family* —" and here Mr. Gough printed *family* on the board in precise round letters " — the letters in this word live together, like a family! Some words are small; some words are big. Small, middle, big, cat, dog, pig!" Mr. Gough grinned, pleased with the rhyme. "Twenty-five-cent question. What do dog, cat and pig have in common?" He paced side to side and slapped his palm with his yardstick. "Hint. They have two things in common."

No one answered.

Gough stopped and scanned the class. "No? I will tell you what they have in common. I will answer myself. I will earn that twenty-five cents. Cats, dogs and pigs are all animals. And they are all small words! Hog, log, bog. Fig, dig, wig!" He pulled a quarter from his left pocket with his left hand, gave it to his right hand and put it into his right pocket. "Now. We see what happens when letters get together. Forty-cent question. What happens when words get together?" He paced and slapped his palm. "Skog."

Ivor shook his head and shrugged.

Again Mr. Gough stopped pacing. Again he made a great show of frowning. He strode down the aisle — slacks hissing — to where Ivor hid at the end of the row.

"Skog." Mr. Gough nodded knowingly. "I had a memo about you this morning. A memo from the principal pinned to the class list, re *Skog, Ivor*. Yes," Mr. Gough nodded as if to assure Ivor it was all true. "It seems you are a two-time loser, Skog. In Grade One for the third time. And you're a skulker. The Skulker Skog."

Jack watched Mr. Gough invite the class to share his satisfaction with this nickname. The class dutifully responded with loud laughter.

"The Skulker Skog," repeated Mr. Gough.

Jack thought Mr. Gough was like the Mountie who'd finally got his man. From where he sat, Jack saw chalk dust on the back of Mr. Gough's pants where he'd brushed against the blackboard. Jack wondered why the blackboard was called the blackboard when it was green.

"There will be no skulking in this class, Skog." Mr. Gough rapped Ivor's desk with his yardstick. "Now, what happens when words get together?"

Ivor blinked as if hypnotized and shrugged again.

Mr. Gough made a performance of imitating Ivor's shrug. "Do you mean you don't know?"

Ivor nodded.

"You mean you do know."

"No."

Mr. Gough corrected him. "No, *sir*."

"I don't know, sir."

"Repeat after me, Skog. *I am an idiot*."

"I am an idiot."

"Sir."

"Sir."

Jack knew Ivor was already plotting to spit in Mr. Gough's underpants.

Jack had first seen Ivor Skog in the change room at the swimming pool with his brother Egbert and that's what they were both doing — working their way along the lockers, opening them up, pulling out people's underpants and spitting in them. The second time Jack saw him, Ivor was on the back porch dunking celery into a jar of mayonnaise while wearing white socks on his hands. Jack had been watching the house for weeks, ever since Miss Funt died, knowing that someone new would be moving in. No one new had ever moved onto his block before and no one had ever died except Olivia Edson's poodle. When Jack saw Ivor with socks on his hands he went down the back porch steps and through the carport, stepped over the strip of grass running down the middle of the alley, jumped the ditch and climbed onto the bottom rail of Miss Funt's fence and called, "Miss Funt cut slugs in half with a knife."

Ivor stopped eating. "What're slugs?"

Jack climbed over the fence and toeing up some sod exposed a long black slug. Ivor came over with his celery and mayonnaise, wiped his mouth with his socked hand and studied the slug.

"There's none o' them in Edmonton."

"Where's Edmonton?"

Ivor frowned and looked around as if trying to spot Edmonton. "Up north."

Jack nodded and repeated to himself, Up north. There was up north, down south, back east and out west.

Ivor said, "Wanna see my warts?"

Jack didn't know anyone with warts. Ivor tugged the socks from his hands. It turned out Ivor had fifty-six warts on the backs of his hands and they came in all shapes and sizes and some even had names. The biggest was called George and was on the back of his right thumb. Ivor told Jack how his mother had applied Compound W to his warts and made him wear the socks to stop him chewing them.

✄

Now Jack watched Ivor anxiously begin chewing George. Mr. Gough slapped Ivor's thumb away from his mouth.

"Nine years old and sucking your thumb, Skog."

Disgusted, Mr. Gough returned to the front of the room and resumed swinging his yardstick as if hacking the heads off his enemies. "What happens when words get together?"

Jack didn't know what happened when words got together and he didn't care. Too nervous to sit still, he bounced his feet, knees pumping up and down. He was too busy to go to school. He had things to do, like collect pop bottles, like visit Rat Gardecki's gas station and watch him raise cars on the hoist, like steal fruit. There was so much fruit. The first fruit of the year was salmonberries. Then came thimbleberries then huckleberries then strawberries and raspberries then apples and plums and blueberries and salal and finally, now, right now, blackberries, the best fruit of all, as black and sweet as syrup in the hot sun. They were out there waiting for him. And of course he had to help the garbage men. Once a week the garbage men came up the alley, one driving, one following on foot, and

Jack was always waiting. The garbage man always showed Jack his latest find, a shoe tree, a knife, a silver fork. Jack wanted to be a garbage man because they got to ride around on the truck's rear bumper. But best of all was visiting Antoine and his thirty-six canaries, something that Jack did alone, without Ivor, without anyone, because Antoine was Jack's special friend. Jack visited Antoine every afternoon and helped open the cages to let the birds fly about the room and get their exercise. Birds needed their exercise. Except now the canaries had all flown away. They were in the plum tree and Antoine was sick, maybe too sick to catch them. Jack would have to get a net and catch the canaries and return them to their cages so Antoine wouldn't worry. Would Antoine be blind now? Jack had seen a blind man with a dog. Maybe Antoine would get a dog.

Jack took his pencil and tried drawing a dog but couldn't, so he drew a swastika instead. Ivor had taught him how to draw swastikas, saying it would protect them against the evil eye. The evil eye came from gypsies. Jack thought swastikas looked like starfish with broken legs. He'd seen starfish at the beach.

Mr. Gough walked up and down the aisles. "When words get together they form what?" He came to Jack's desk. Jack put his pencil down and looked up. Mr. Gough was staring. For a moment Jack thought Mr. Gough was going to praise his swastikas. Instead he plucked Jack's notebook.

"What is this?" He looked from the notebook to Jack to the notebook again. "Do you know what this is?"

Jack heard his own voice, small and far away, "A swastika."

"A swastika ... A *swastika*! And do you know what a swastika *is*? Do you know what a swastika *means*?"

"No."

"No?" Mr. Gough was astounded.

"No, sir."

"No, sir?" Mr. Gough was even more astounded. He rapped the page with his finger. It made a popping sound. "A lot of my friends died because of this and here you sit merrily doodling away. You. Klein. A Jew!" Mr. Gough ripped the page from the notebook and crushed it. Then, still staring at Jack but addressing the class, he announced, "There will be no swastikas here. None. Ever. Is that understood?"

Heart beating like an alarm bell, Jack watched Mr. Gough return to the front of the room and drop the crumpled paper into the green metal bin by his desk. Jack was a *Joo*. What was a *Joo*?

Mr. Gough exhaled hard as if exhausted, the way Jack's dad sometimes did when he came home from work. "One last time, what happens when words get together?"

Jack kept his head down close to the grey Formica desk. At the top right corner was a hole for an ink bottle. In Grade One only pencils were allowed. Mr. Gough had already told them they'd have to wait until Grade Three before advancing to pens. Jack reached toward the hole and fit his hand into it — and got stuck. He felt the same air-sucking horror he had the time he got his head stuck between the fence slats.

"Do you mean I am going to get this forty-cent question, too? Sentences! Words join hands to make sentences!"

The bell rang.

The yardstick slammed the desk.

Mr. Gough pointed. "Recess. Fifteen-cent question. Who can tell me our room number?"

"One-oh-two."

"Correct!" Mr. Gough pointed his yardstick at Miriam. "That is correct, Miriam. Miriam is correct."

Miriam smiled proudly. Her fluffy pink dress looked more suited to a birthday party than school. She had a red ribbon in her hair that matched her red shoes.

"Did you all hear that? One-oh-two. One-*zero*-two." Mr. Gough wrote 102 on the board with such dash his chalk broke and bounced on the floor. "How else would you know what room to return to after recess?" He shook his head as if they were ninnies. He found a new stick of chalk on the ledge and underlined 102. Again the chalk broke and bounced. Mr. Gough paid no attention. "The bell will ring again in twenty minutes. That is your signal to come back." He strode to the door crunching chunks of chalk under his black shoes. "This row. Single file. Hup!"

Hand stuck in the ink hole, Jack watched Mr. Gough touch each child's shoulder as he or she passed, as if he was wishing them good luck as they parachuted from the room. Out the door they went one after another. When Ivor Skog was about to jump Mr. Gough pinched the hair at Ivor's temple and hoisted him high onto his toes so that Ivor looked like he was dangling from a hook.

"The Skulker Skog." Mr. Gough shook Ivor amiably. "Let me tell you a little secret, Skog. I like fellows like you. And I'll tell you why — because you're a problem, and I like to solve problems. I intend to solve you. Who knows," said Gough, reflecting, "it is not entirely impossible that we might even be friends. Someday you — yes you, Skog — will return to this room and seek me out to thank me." With that, he pushed Ivor into the hall.

When it was Jack's row's turn the floor tipped side to side and Jack felt seasick. He stood — hand still stuck — and watched those in front of him file forward. When it was his turn the other kids waited and watched. Dizzy, Jack nearly fell over. Mr. Gough would give him the strap for this. Ivor had warned Jack about the strap. Some straps were long and wide and made of leather, others were wood. Ivor remembered one strap that was not a strap at all but a ping-pong bat named Oscar. *Who wants to say hello to Oscar?* the teacher would ask. Ivor said the strap stung. It was like boiling water, it was like fire. The boy behind nudged Jack. He tugged at his stuck hand like a fox in a trap. The boy nudged him again, but Jack's hand stayed stuck. Finally the boy stepped on by and the others followed, filing past with gleeful glances at Jack's crisis. Finally everyone was out the door and it was only him and Mr. Gough.

"Jack."

Anchored to his desk, Jack looked at his hand and then at Mr. Gough and with all his strength clenched his muscles so as not to pee.

When Mr. Gough grasped the problem he seemed to relax. He slid his hands into his own pockets and jingled his change and shook his head. He ambled on over to Jack and, after standing there a moment as if enjoying himself, pulled one hand from his pocket and raised it high. Jack followed it. It was so big it blocked the ceiling light. It hovered there, a vast hand spread like a hawk or a bat that now began to descend to catch him in its claws. But instead of attacking him, Mr. Gough's hand came to rest gently on Jack's skull. Jack felt Mr. Gough's fingers testing his skull the way he'd seen his mother test melons. He thought of the crushed melon he'd seen on the floor of the Woodward's produce department, all red and wet and mushed.

"Jack," said Mr. Gough. "Jack, Jack, Jack."

All Jack could see was the tip of Mr. Gough's gold tie that came to a point and made Jack think of a sword, like the one owned by the genie in Aladdin's lamp. Jack's lunch box was an Aladdin's lamp lunch box, though if you rubbed it no genie appeared.

"You're having a rough day, aren't you? Swastikas, a stuck hand and on top of that you were late this morning. First day of school — first day of your new life — and you arrived late." Mr. Gough pondered the enormity of this failure. "What if your father was late? Think of it. He'd lose his job. If he lost his job he'd have no money. If he had no money you'd be on the street."

From Jack's perspective Mr. Gough's nostrils looked like holes dug under a stump. Mr. Gough smelled of chalk and Brylcreem. *A little dab'll do ya.* That's what it said on the TV.

Gazing into Jack's eyes, Mr. Gough whispered coaxingly, "Think of it, Jack. Think of it. On the street, no food, no clothes, no house."

Hand still stuck in the ink hole, Jack tried imagining no house. Jack's father loved their house, Jack's mother hated the house, and Antoine lived in the basement of their house, except that now Antoine was sick and his canaries — all thirty-six of them — had flown away and Jack had to get them back.

5

Clocks and Bridges

Waiting at a red light, Ray patted on Old Spice, then slotted the bottle back in the leather-covered compartment in the armrest. It made his neck sting, but Charlene had bought it for him, winking and saying the smell got her going. Ray liked that. He recalled Zsa Zsa Gabor's formula for a happy marriage: *Every man should have a mistress.* Looking in the rearview he peeled the scab of toilet paper from his throat then dabbed at the red mark with a wet fingertip. He was still sweating. He said aloud, "Thanks, Lorraine." He couldn't meet Charlene with sweat stains under his arms. He needed a new shirt, a mickey of Wiser's, plus he had to get to a phone and call in sick.

There was Rat Gardecki over at the Viking Service Station filling a Studebaker. He was wearing his green uniform and hat. Rat in his hat, like that Dr. Seuss book of Jacko's. Ray knew Rat loved that uniform and kept it spotless. It included a jacket with a crest that said: ROLAND. Ray suspected it reminded Rat of his air force days. Corporal Roland Gardecki, Royal Canadian Air Force. Ray understood. The best time of his life, even though Rat was not a pilot but part of the ground crew. Now the closest Rat Gardecki got to airplanes was building balsa wood models with miniature gas-powered engines that he flew in the park. Rat was always talking about getting on at the airport and working on the big babies. He knew all about what Boeing was up to down in Seattle, and he followed the space race between the Yanks and Russkies.

Now Gardecki spotted Ray and offered a jaunty wave, like a salute. Ray responded with a light beep-beep on the horn. Had he seen him slapping on the Old Spice? Would he invent some story and tell that cow Olivia? Ray knew how Rat Gardecki's mind worked. The slightest thing made him suspicious. If you didn't fill the tank he concluded you were tightening your belt because you were on the brink of financial collapse. When Ray bought the Thunderbird, Gardecki decided Ray'd won the Irish Sweepstakes, got a big promotion, or scored on the stock market. He'd been all buddy-buddy: *You're a Jew, Ray, how 'bout a stock tip?* Ray had wanted to shoot back, *You're a wop, Rat, how 'bout putting in a good word with the mafia for me?* ... Another thing that peeved Ray was how their names, Ray and Rat, were only a letter apart. If they got to be chums it'd be Ray'n' Rat this,

Rat'n' Ray that. So he kept his distance.

Still, Ray conceded Rat Gardecki had two things going for him: he liked Jack and he admired the Thunderbird. The man had taste in cars if not in women. The subject of Rat and Olivia was one area where Ray and Lorraine always shared a laugh. She brought him Olivia gossip and he brought her Rat tales. His imitation of Rat's side-of-the-mouth banter never failed to get a grin. *Goddamn it Ray, I hear Sinatra's got two of these babies, a white one with red interior and a red one with white interior. Lemme tell you something: you can keep your Rolls and your Mercedes. I'll take a T-bird hands down any day of the week, my friend, any day ...* Rat understood — from a professional point of view — that this was no ordinary car but a prestige vehicle, something to take pride in. Yet no way Ray would let Gardecki get his mitts on the Bird's motor. Not a chance. When time came for its first tune-up he'd make an appointment with Western Ford on Seymour Street. He knew Rat's beak would be bent out of shape over that, but with the cost of this car he wouldn't entrust it to anyone but the best. Sitting at the light, it occurred to Ray that Rat probably had his own theories about Monsieur Antoine Gaudin and his canaries and that the next time he pulled in to gas up he should ask.

The light changed, Ray stepped on the gas, the Bird glided. The sleek, smooth flow calmed him. It was gorgeous. It was aerodynamic and elegant as only a '65 Thunderbird could be. Ray ordered his tasks: telephone call, mickey of rye, new shirt, bing, bang, boom, one, two, three. Lack of organization, that's why guys got nabbed. System, you had to have a system.

Ray caught people in other cars checking out the Thunderbird. He draped his left wrist over the red steering wheel and felt good. A quality car like this was a yacht — you didn't drive, you sailed — and it brought out the best in him. It was medicine; all he had to do was sit in it and he felt better. That was engineering at its finest. He'd heard about some country in Africa — Ghana or Gabon or Guinea — where they didn't bury people in boxes but in coffins designed to look like their favourite cars. He was all for it. "Bury me in my Bird," sang Ray, turning on the radio. Even the thick click of the zinc knob said quality. He thought of the men who worked on the Thunderbird line at Ford. They weren't workers, they were craftsmen, and that wasn't a job — it was a position. Ray had studied all the manuals that came with the car and kept them in the glove box in their original plastic sleeves.

The radio was set to Top Dog 98. The 8:30 news. Ray turned it up. Eighteen straight days and no rain. Today was also Wacky Bennett's birthday. The big six-five for the premier of B.C. India and Pakistan were dropping bombs on each other. Albert Schweitzer was in a coma. Ray hummed "Fly me to the Moon."

Either that or drive me to Las Vegas, he thought. Ray dreamed of cruising down south to Vegas to catch the Rat Pack at Caesar's Palace. While the kids were busy choosing their favourite Beatle, Ray Klein was picking his favourite Rat Packer. It was tricky. He opted for a combination: Dino's looks, Sammy's cool, Frank's command; but if he had to choose he might surprise them all and go for Peter Lawford. There was something about that British accent and those sideburns. Lawford was married to

Jack Kennedy's sister. Lawford was suave, possessing a European sophistication absent in Dino's wolfish leer, subtler than Sammy's cool and a full notch above Frank's street-smart style. Frank was too bony, too crude, with a touch of the wop about him — something Dino had risen above. As for Sammy, he was up there with Nat King Cole — one of the good ones. Ray had even read Sammy's autobiography, *Yes, I Can.* Ray could relate to it; he too had faced prejudice. And Joey Bishop? What could you say about a Jew with a Catholic name? Not that Ray didn't understand an entertainer was a special case, that you had to consider the audience, and that — as his dad used to warn him — goys will be goys, so be careful, watch your ass. It occurred to Ray how some people really did look like their stage names. Tony Curtis, for example, looked more like a Tony Curtis than a Bernie Schwartz. Even that dirty bugger Lenny Bruce didn't look like an Alfred Schneider. Ray thought of changing his name to Ray Lawford. That would make Lorraine, Lorraine Lawford. It had a ring. He knew what she'd have to say about that — *It's stupid, Ray* — so he never mentioned it. Rat Gardecki liked it when Ray called him Rat Pack Gardecki. He smiled and winked, *You got it, Ray boy, you got it, my man.*

Ray pressed the cigarette lighter and tapped up a Rothman's. He loved the smell of a freshly opened pack of smokes. He loved the smell of the foil and the tobacco and the feel of the raised lettering on the pack. The lighter popped out and Ray lit up. That was another thing, Lorraine said he smoked so much he tasted like an ashtray. Charlene, on the other hand, liked smoking. Charlene was also into going to Vegas. Lorraine laughed whenever he mentioned Vegas. Charlene wanted to do watercolours of the Nevada desert. Ray's Vegas fantasy involved doing it in the Bird with the top down under that desert sky. Charlene would kneel above him all naked and pink and she'd call him Dino, or Sammy, or better yet, *Peter*. Later — gowned and tuxedoed — they'd catch the midnight show at Caesar's Palace, get a table right up front where they could hob with the nobs, wink and smile, sip scotch and water, snap their fingers and — while the roulette wheels turned and the dice tumbled — admire the shine of Sammy's conk.

Ray teased the gas pedal and felt those cylinders surge. As usual that woke his John Thomas. He opened his legs to give the lad room to stretch. He recalled Europe in '46, growing simultaneously aroused and embarrassed by what those German women would do for an Oh Henry bar or a pack of smokes. Most of his buddies said given what Adolph had done, the *frauleins* deserved whatever they got. Ray agreed, sort of. He was careful never to tell any of the women his last name because it would only complicate things and Ray liked things simple. That's why he'd enjoyed being in the army: the routine, the organization, the system.

While on leave he'd visited France and, among other places, the region of Lorraine. Ten years later he met Lorraine in Vancouver at the Aristocratic. He still recalled every detail of that evening. It was the supper hour rush and she was a waitress, but she still managed to find time to lean on the counter and study her high-school French. She was timid and remote. Ray would never admit it to anyone, but he often felt the same, so he was encouraged. She had a great figure, sandy hair, wide-spaced blue eyes, a few freckles. She was a *goy*, a *shiksa*, and that was good because he didn't like the way Jews sniffed you out and assumed some bond, like Nancy Levin dogging him in Grade 12, figuring it was only natural that they date. Or Lou Kovitsch who always looked at Ray with those self-conscious eyes like they shared something, like they were in some sort of secret club. Lou Kovitsch was a dick.

That day Ray had asked in his own clumsy French if she'd ever been to France.

She'd looked at him to scrutinize his sincerity. Was this just another come-on? After a moment, she said, with a stylized French pout he could tell she'd picked up from the movies, *"Non. Mais, aussitot que j'aurai l'argent."*

It took Ray a few frantic moments to interpret. *No, but I'll go as soon as I have the money.* He nodded, impressed not just at her plan but her air of determination. "Paris?"

"Oui, et Dieppe et tout le pays."

"Comment t'appelles-tu?"

"Je m'appelle Lorraine. Et toi?"

His French about tapped, he shifted to English. "Ray. Good to meet you."

They shook hands. When she smiled he almost whimpered. He figured he could bask forever in the glow of that smile. It was like spring sun on winter grass. The image embarrassed him. Jesus, here he was getting all poetic. When she smiled her wary eyes lost their fear and Ray was flattered. It turned out she knew a lot about France and the war and in particular about the retreat from Dieppe. She also knew about the history of the region of Lorraine.

"Lorraine. That's you."

She shrugged and laughed.

"So tell me."

"Well," she occupied her hands rearranging the salt and pepper, "in 843 Louis the Pious divided the region of Lorraine between his three sons."

"Louis the Pious."

"Then there were all the kings named Charles," said Lorraine.

"Charles."

"Charles the Fat, Charles the Simple and Charles the Bald."

"Fat, simple and bald."

They were both laughing now.

"And there was Conrad the Red, Godfrey the Bearded and Godfrey the Hunchback."

"Red, bearded and hunchbacked," said Ray. "Sound like great-looking guys." He teased her, but he was impressed. He was intrigued that she should know such things.

Ray was thirty-one at the time — getting on — and not just single but lonely, another thing he wouldn't have admitted to anyone. He made a point of coming around to the restaurant more regularly. Ray liked the fact that Lorraine was younger than he was. She was raw material and that meant he could shape her; they'd mesh like finely machined gears. They could have a good relationship, a good marriage and a good family. He knew so many guys who'd hooked up with women who were already set in their ways and there was nothing but trouble.

Their first date he took her to *We're No Angels* with Humphrey Bogart, Peter Ustinov and Aldo Ray, a comedy about three good-hearted cons who escape Devil's Island and descend upon the home of a bankrupt merchant whom they end up saving. Lorraine loved the tropical setting, though she hated the dimwit daughter and the mother.

The intensity of Lorraine's reaction to the mother surprised him. "Why don't you like her?"

"She read her daughter's diary!"

"Did yours?"

She didn't answer right away.

They were sitting in a different Aristocratic, on the corner of Broadway and Granville. It was Saturday night and cars rolled past in the rain: Buick, Ford, Chrysler. Ray was driving a Chevy Bel Air at the time. He made sure it was parked where he could keep an eye on it.

"Slick and shiny as sucked candies," mused Lorraine, chin on her hand, watching the cars pass.

It sounded to Ray as if she was quoting a line of poetry. He nodded politely.

"Tell me about France, about Paris."

What did she want to hear? It hadn't been exotic, it had been old and dirty and tired. He didn't want to let her down, though, so described Notre Dame, the narrow streets, the old men fishing along the banks of the Seine. "People cried a lot. They looked relieved."

She nodded, as if that made sense. Then for some reason she told him about *her* reading her *mother's* diary, not the other way around. "My mother didn't care enough about anyone else to be curious."

At the time it struck Ray as the profound observation of a woman who had to grow up fast. Yet now, years later, Lorraine wasn't maturing as he'd expected. She wasn't womanly or serene. She didn't bake or do her nails. In fact, she seemed to be reverting to adolescence. When he told her Vancouver was the safest place in the world she said maybe a little danger was healthy. He'd asked her what the hell that meant. Were they supposed to move to L.A. where they were having race riots? Vietnam? Africa?

And just what was her thing about the Bird and the house and Vegas? She was laughing at him and it pissed him off. Who did she think she was? He'd been in the army, he had a good job, he paid the bills. Hell, he'd been working since he was twelve. What was funny about that? Ray's father had been bedridden for the last twenty years of his life, so Ray had had to pitch in and help his mother scrub other people's houses. Charlene understood this and never laughed at him — she respected him. Maybe if Lorraine gave him a little more respect he wouldn't be on his way to Charlene's right now.

Then there were Lorraine's moods. She'd be sullen and giddy and snide in the space of a minute. Ray never knew what was coming out of her mouth next and it was getting worse. It wasn't just this France kick, it was more than that. A lot of the kids these days were in on it. He wondered if Frank Sinatra had these problems with Mia Farrow. Something was going on and Ray didn't know what. Maybe there was truth to the talk in the papers about fluoridation being a Commie plot.

Ray signalled left — the ping of the light on the dash flashing with aeronautic precision — and cruised down Commercial Drive. He often made this little detour en route to Charlene's so he could check out the old neighbourhood and show off the car. It was an indulgence, but the Bird did that to him, made him feel roguish and bold. He passed Manitoba Hardware, Bufton's Flowers, the Gran Sasso where the Italians danced on weekends. He thought of the Italians as a nation of long-shoremen, short, burly, hairy and loud, always hollering like they were deaf, jabbing their thick fingers in each other's faces. As a kid you knew exactly where you stood: you were a wop or a ricer or a bohunk or a Hebe. You called each other all kinds of names, but at the same time everyone got along, everyone was together, because it was the 1930s and no one had anything, which meant no one was a threat. You swam in Rain Lake, played soccer with a ball of rags, shot rats with slingshots down by the grain elevators. But when it came to girls you stayed with your own. Not that any of them had ever looked twice at coat-hanger shouldered Ray when he was in school.

He slowed down as he passed Britannia Senior Secondary, his alma mater. There they were, clusters of girls, haughty, laughing, hugging their books, tossing their hair and feigning indifference. One more year of school then out in the world. In two years many would be pushing strollers. That's what had happened to Lorraine.

Her plans had fallen through because she met him. It was his fault in a way, and he knew that in her heart she blamed him for the fact that she'd never made it to France. Yet was it his fault they fell in love? Did love have fault? Ray argued — like Perry Mason in the courtroom — that she — *she!* — was the one who'd proposed to him! Talk about bold. Talk about brazen. She'd said she felt for him the way Desdemona felt for Othello: "She loved me for the dangers I had passed." Jesus ... Ray had never had much use for plays or poetry, but he'd gone and read *Othello* after Lorraine said that; it frightened the hell out of him. Lorraine was one serious piece of work. It made him re-evaluate her, made him realize the war and everything he'd been through meant something to her. She packed around a whole inner world, like a house with hidden rooms, secret corridors, attics and cellars. He figured it had to do with her old man. She went on and on about him. It probably had a lot to do with her mother in the asylum, too. Ray had only met Lorraine's mother one time — at their wedding — and that was enough.

Lorraine had agonized over whether or not to even invite her mother. Ray knew she was humiliated, and while Ray never said anything, he worried about whether Lorraine might have inherited Estelle's illness. He was curious to get a look at Estelle and to talk to her, as if to check the fine print of a warranty. In what he imagined to be a discerning bit of diplomacy, he played it cool, sensing Lorraine was feeling him out on the issue.

"Do what you think's right," he'd said. "I'm behind you."

They were walking the Stanley Park seawall at the time, the water's glassy glint stabbing their eyes and Ray's new sandals raising blisters on his heels.

"She hallucinates," Lorraine warned him. "She hears voices. She talks to herself."

"Is she dangerous?"

"Well ..."

Ray began to worry. He wanted the wedding to reflect well on him, especially given that most of the guests were going to be from the office. Old man Selwyn himself would be there. This could affect his future at the firm. He'd planned a straight-forward secular ceremony and a good party afterward with lots of food, wine and scotch.

"Isn't she on anything?"

"Of course she is. Thorazine. She's psychotic."

Psychotic. Ray thought of Anthony Perkins in *Psycho*. He didn't like the sound of this at all. He tried sounding casual. "So, I mean, the stuff works, doesn't it?"

"Most of the time."

Ray lit a cigarette and inhaled deeply. *Most of the time ...* Then he thought of something else. He cleared his throat. "What've you told her?"

"About what?"

"About me."

"I don't know. You're an engineer, you're —"

"Jewish?"

"*No.*" Lorraine was petulant. "She wouldn't care anyway." Suddenly near tears, she said, "She's the only parent either of us have left. She should be there. I want her there. Otherwise she'll make me feel guilty the rest of my life."

"You already feel guilty."

"It'll get worse."

Ray wished his folks could be there, and of course Del, his younger brother. For a guy who'd missed the real action in the war, he thought, I've seen a lot of death. They reached the shaded stretch of the seawall where it approached the Lion's Gate Bridge. Ahead, Burrard Inlet curved between the forested slopes of the North Shore on the left and the city's waterfront on the right. Ray took Lorraine's arm securely in his and said in a sober voice gauged to reassure his young bride-to-be, "She should be there."

Lorraine sounded grateful. "You think so?"

"Yes."

Relieved to have that settled, Ray pointed at the under-structure of the bridge directly above them and told her about Roman arches.

✖

Ray saw his mother-in-law at the ceremony, but they didn't speak until the reception. She looked good, and her composure reassured him. She wore a sky-blue skirt and jacket and a ruffled white blouse, and her dark blonde hair was done like Doris Day's. When they shook hands she smiled and said in a velvety voice, as if they were old friends, "Ray. Good to see you." It almost sounded as if she was the hostess and he was the guest.

"Glad you could make it, Estelle." He'd practised various greetings beforehand, carefully avoiding any words that might hint at her living in a mental hospital. He was relieved that while she was certainly giving him the once over, there didn't seem to be any sniff-out-the-Jew to it.

The reception took place in Dale Reed's rumpus room. Reed was one of Ray's co-workers at Selwyn and had finished the room himself: the floor with lino designed to look like slate, the walls with plywood that looked like cherry, the ceiling panelled in white cork like a dentist's office. The wedding cake, the food and the punch were set out on a paper-covered ping pong table and silver streamers garlanded the ceiling.

Estelle sat by the wall sipping ginger ale and studying Ray. Even from across the room, separated by a dozen people, he felt her gaze. Every time he looked over she was watching him. It felt as if she was peering at him through a telescope. He tried to be understanding. He was marrying her one and only child; naturally she was concerned for her welfare. After a while he saw she was smiling, just the corners of her mouth, as if amused. That worried Ray. Women worried him. You had to be careful because, in his all-too-fleeting experience, they were always thinking things. He went over and asked her how she was doing, causing Estelle to smile even wider.

"Fine."

"Good. Another drink?"

The empty tumbler in her hand rose, though her gaze never left Ray's face. When he returned with the drink, she asked, "How old are you, Ray?"

"Thirty-two."

She nodded. "You're closer to my age than Lorraine's."

Her tone was affable so Ray didn't read too much significance into the statement, though he did feel compelled to observe that Lorraine was mature for her age.

"So was I," responded Estelle with that enigmatic smile.

Ray began to wonder: Were her eyes glazed or penetrating?

Later, Ray tinged a fork against his wine glass and stood to say a few words. There were whistles and applause. Yet Estelle, as if the cue was for her, stepped to the middle of the room and with everyone watching announced calmly, "You're a fool."

Lorraine, trapped in the folds of her wedding dress, said, "Ma —"

"You think you can make this that. That can never be this. It is what it is," said Estelle.

Then she walked out and Lorraine, rustling like a heap of leaves in her white dress, hurried after her. It was an hour before she returned, during which time Ray explained that Estelle had had a breakdown and was on medication. The guests nodded politely. Ray began worrying more than ever that these things did indeed run in the family.

He was still worrying. How much of Estelle — via Lorraine — was in Jack? What would that do to Jack's future? Not that the boy had to be an engineer, though engineering *was* the highest calling. Just look at history. Everything that counted had been built by engineers: aqueducts, dams, smelters. Engineers had pulled people up from the muck and down from the trees and they were still doing it. The train, the car, the plane, the elevator, the toilet, the ballpoint pen. Who built bridges? *English profs?* That, to Ray, was the stuff of movies: *A Bridge Too Far, The Bridge On the River Kwai.*

Ideally, Ray would have liked to go into bridges, but practically speaking industrial engineering was more lucrative, so he'd joined Selwyn and focused on the lumber industry, redesigning mill systems. Still, on winter evenings he'd pour himself a rye and seven and unroll his pet project on the kitchen table: plans to connect the Mainland and Vancouver Island, a distance of approximately twenty-five miles depending upon location. It was a visionary project, one whose time had not yet come, but most definitely would. The English were discussing a cross-channel bridge or tunnel. The Japanese were planning to connect the main island of Honshu with the northern island of Hokkaido. If they could do it so could he. Ray studied aerial photos and maps of the Gulf of Georgia, and as the Vancouver rain raged down around him he considered options: a combination tunnel and a series of linked pontoons, a causeway, or one vast span arching all the way across like a goddamn iron rainbow with his name on it in bronze letters: RAYMOND S. KLEIN BRIDGE.

Ray's many maps gave him various views of Vancouver and its environs. The city proper lay wedged between Burrard Inlet to the north and the Fraser River to the south, butted up against the Gulf of Georgia to the west. As Ray leaned over his maps and his charts, Jack occasionally joined him, intrigued by whatever it was that so absorbed his father. On one of those occasions Jack announced that Vancouver looked like a dragon. Ray, curious, leaned to see from Jack's point of view.

"What're you talking about?"

Jack pointed. The city was its skull, the dragon's jaws were the north and south arms of the Fraser, Lulu Island was its tongue, and the body was the river itself, snaking down from the interior westward to the sea. Ray stared. He blinked once, twice, then saw Jack was right, the river was its throat and intestine and the whole thing was slithering into the ocean with Stanley Park jutting like a horn from the top of its head. All in all, a very Oriental-looking dragon, and U.B.C., his old school, was its snout. After that, Ray never looked at a map of Vancouver the same way again.

Ray didn't tell any of his colleagues at Selwyn Engineering about his bridge plan. It was his baby and he didn't want anyone else muscling in. He followed all the developments in Vancouver's urban planning department and kept a scrapbook of any articles on the subject. When the time was right he'd be there and the whole city, the whole country — all North America — would know his name. Maybe he'd even write a book about it.

He'd make his father proud. While Ray had been growing up, his father was virtually bedridden, barely able to walk, much less work, his lungs gassed to rags in World War I. His dad's voice was a wheeze so that everything he said sounded like his last words, giving them a desperate and prophetic tone. When he talked in his sleep, as he often did, he spoke in the Yiddish he'd learned as a child in Montreal. Ray often heard him because the house was so small. He'd frown in the dark as he listened to the German-sounding language coming out of this stranger in the next room. It was scary. When Ray asked him about the Yiddish, his father insisted Ray was the one dreaming.

If Ray had bridges, his father had had clocks and watches, all kinds, broken mostly. Ray and his mother used to find them and give them to him to fix. Neighbours came by to exchange a jar of jam or a pair of socks for his expertise.

One day his father pried the back off a pocket watch with the point of a jackknife and invited Ray to admire the intricate world of twitching gears. That's what Ray's father had loved about clocks: they were a world unto themselves that you could control and comprehend. Side-by-side, shoulder-to-shoulder, they'd gazed into that watch, his dad pointing to the various components: main wheel, first pinion, spindle, second wheel. The memory of that day still brought Ray to tears. His father — frail, helpless, reliant — was the reason he'd become an engineer.

6

Je mourrais

The older cop wanted to use the phone, so Lorraine led them upstairs to the kitchen. She sat at the table with her hands between her knees, stared at the tabletop and thought about Antoine carrying her photograph in his wallet.

She knew the photo. Ray had taken it on the grounds of the Empress Hotel while they were on holiday in Victoria last year. Antoine must have stolen it. He must have come up during the day while she was out. She found it nearly impossible to imagine him doing anything even remotely underhanded. But clearly he'd opened the back door, entered the bedroom, gone through the drawers in her bureau and found the album with the Eiffel

Tower in gold relief on the leather cover. He would have paged through the album, seen the wedding photos, the snaps of Jack, Estelle, the few existing shots of Ray's parents and his brother Del. What else did he look at? Did he check the closet? Sit on the bed? Think about her? She imagined his clean hands with their perfect nails touching her underwear. She imagined him discovering himself in the oval mirror above the bureau. What went through his mind at the moment he saw himself framed there in the glass? She would have told him it was okay, he could have anything he wanted. Anything. It seemed so unlike the calm and balanced Antoine she knew. "Why didn't you ask?" she said aloud.

"Excuse me?" The cop covered the receiver with his hand and looked at her.

"Nothing. Sorry."

He raised the receiver and resumed his conversation. "Yeah. Looks like a suicide. Uh-huh. Gonna need a photographer."

Lorraine's breath rushed from her chest. "Photographer?" Appalled, she rose from her chair. "No!"

The cop looked at her, raised eyebrows laddering his forehead with wrinkles. He shook his head meaning it was out of Lorraine's hands.

She stared at the crushed blue marble pattern on the tabletop. What had possessed them to buy such an ugly pattern? The day she met Antoine, he said it looked like shattered glass pressed under a roller. That was November fourteenth, 1963; she remembered the date because it was just eight days before John Kennedy was killed and the rain had been falling for two weeks, foreshadowing the grim winter months to come. She'd lived in Vancouver all her life and yet with each year she was less capable of coping with the rain. Ray said she was being melodramatic. But each November the darkness enclosed her: clay-grey clouds, bare black trees, damp walls, rotting fences, wet tarmac, flowing sewers, overflowing ditches and drizzle dripping through endless afternoons, day after day, week after week, all winter long, the only brightness the neon signs reflected off the water rushing along the gutters and gleaming on wet cars.

The "For Rent" sign had been up since the start of the month and Ray was getting cranky because no one had inquired. Then Antoine knocked. Lorraine opened the front door to an elderly man of average height in a charcoal suit with a white shirt open at the collar. Her first impression was that he wasn't from around here; he was from far away. For one thing, when he removed his hat he revealed long white hair, not oiled and slicked back but clean and luxuriant. His shoulders were wet, but he was smiling and smelled faintly of parsley. She liked that. Behind him the rain overflowed the eavestrough and it was as if he'd emerged from a waterfall. She was doing her toenails at the time and had cotton plugs between her toes.

"Excuse me." She laughed and invited him in, then retreated to the bathroom where she plucked the plugs and blew on her toenails. She appraised herself in the mirror. Why did she care? He was an old man. Except he wasn't, he was different and she knew it. She led him via the kitchen door onto the back porch, down the wooden stairs and around to the ground floor suite where, once inside, he immediately spotted the poster of Sacré-Coeur. Lorraine had put up the poster to make the suite more attractive. Antoine pointed out a café in the bottom right corner called *Au Gras Normand.*

"Incredible!" He looked at her, smiling, and said he knew the owner, a man who wore a Danish squirrel fur toupée and claimed to have been in the Resistance.

"Squirrel fur?"

"*Danish* squirrel fur."

Lorraine loved it. For the next hour they sat at the kitchen table talking and laughing and discussing France. His English was grammatically perfect though occasionally an accent rippled through. France was *Fronzs* or sometimes *Frentz.* To delay his departure, Lorraine invited him upstairs and made lunch, tuna fish and mayonnaise on white bread, apologizing for such bland fare even as Antoine insisted it was delicious. He seemed happy to stay on and she was glad he did. Stuck at home, she was easy prey to visits from Olivia. Antoine's presence was like having the world come to her. When he'd knocked she'd already done the breakfast dishes, mopped the floors, thought about what to make for supper, had a load in the machine and had been reading *Madame Bovary* while waiting for her toenails to dry. It was her third run at *Madame Bovary,* and as with the previous two attempts she was forever shoving it aside due to an overwhelming claustrophobia. It was a bleak book with a dull heroine, two opinions she was certain proved her ignorance. She debated whether to display the book to show off her sophistication, or hide it in case

Antoine questioned her and discovered her shallowness. Leading the way into the kitchen, she'd stashed it on the shelf amid the spice tins, but Antoine spotted it anyway.

He blew air scornfully and shook his head. "*Madame Woe is Me*, by Gasbag Blowhard."

Lorraine laughed at the cheek.

"I'm wrong?" Antoine grinned, cool grey eyes gleaming with flecks of gold at the edges. He had good teeth, high cheekbones, a thin nose and sharp chin.

What a relief. She continued to laugh, and when he finally inquired about the rent Lorraine thought for only an instant before cutting it by a third. "It's fifty dollars a month," she said, fearing that it was still too high. He nodded but looked concerned, causing her to panic. "Too much?"

"No, no. But I have baird."

Baird? He wanted room and board?

He coughed and apologized. "*Birds*. Canaries. Thirty-six," he said, voice flat and clear.

"Thirty-six canaries?"

"And I let them fly loose. My room is their room."

Lorraine imagined a suite full of birds and fell in love.

When she showed him the rental contract Ray had drawn up, Antoine took a moment to read it over.

"Klein."

"Yes."

He looked up, considering her for a moment — Lorraine becoming self-conscious, her hand rising out of habit to her hair, then the thought occurring to her that Antoine was Jewish, that there was a bond. He nodded and signed and counted out the cash. They shook hands, his as warm and dry as a brick in the sun, and strolled onto the front porch where he took a moment to stare at the rain.

"Do you want to reconsider and move to Mexico?" Lorraine asked.

"I don't mind rain."

Lorraine shivered and hugged herself. "I do."

"It's clean."

"It turns everything to mud."

"Flowers grow in mud." He laughed as if embarrassed. He had a resonant laugh that came from his nose. He touched his hat and went down the street, hands clasped behind his back like an Old World philosopher pacing the cobbled lanes of some Eastern European city. She noticed he was slightly pigeon-toed. Where was he staying? Only after he was gone did she think to tell him he didn't have to wait until the end of the month to move in. He could move in now, today.

That evening Ray said, "He Jewed you down!"

"*Ray!*"

"*Fifty?*"

"In two weeks not one person's even looked," she said.

"The rent's seventy-five."

"We've got a good tenant."

"Right. Lorraine the psychologist."

"I can tell."

"You can tell. Right."

"I can," she insisted. She had a good feeling about him.

"He rooked you."

"You're paranoid."

Wearily, Ray said, "I'll have to talk to him."

"No. It's done, Ray. He signed the contract."

"Thanks to you."

Lorraine marked the days until Antoine was to move in. He was back on the morning of December first in a taxi with two suitcases, a trunk and six birdcages each containing six canaries. *Six times six is thirty-six.* The first numbers in the times table that Jack would memorize.

✄

Now Jack was in Grade One and all that was left of Antoine were those cages. Lorraine felt the muscles in her face stiffen to a frown. He'd abandoned her. Right here, downstairs, within twenty feet. *I'd have given you a photo! I'd have given you anything!* Hadn't he seen that she wanted him? Wasn't a younger woman every older man's fantasy? Saturday evening Lorraine even told him, casually but pointedly, that she was on the Pill and meant to stay on it.

His only reaction had been a polite nod.

"I'm not getting pregnant again," she'd said. "It was like being a prisoner in my own body." They were drinking wine seated on a blanket beneath the plum tree. Ray was at his reunion.

"But wasn't being pregnant an adventure?"

That had caught her by surprise. "Well, sure. Of course," she said quickly. "It's just that —"

"It's traumatic." Antoine nodded his understanding.

"Your body's not yours anymore."

"Still, I'd love to get pregnant," he said.

What a thing to say, but somehow typical of Antoine. She thought of pregnant men wandering about in floral muumuus with backaches and morning sickness. Ray had viewed her body as an ingenious piece of technology, though he'd shuddered at the thought of even being in the delivery room.

"Why not?" asked Antoine. "What is there in a man's life that can compare? Nothing. Nothing at all. To bring someone into the world instead of taking them out of it."

"You could have been an, I mean ..." Lorraine stumbled. She didn't know what to say. "Obstetricians. They give life."

Antoine wasn't convinced.

Lorraine glimpsed an immense sense of loss. The war? Bachelorhood? The regrets of an aging and solitary man?

"I guess on good days I felt part of something, you know, bigger," she said. "On bad days," she shrugged, "like a host for some," she grew embarrassed, "some *creature,* as if my body had been colonized." Antoine frowned so she changed the subject. To lighten the mood she rolled her eyes and chuckled. "Of course, I had to deal with Ray." She generally avoided the subject of Ray while with Antoine, but now and then he came in handy as comic relief. She described how, to gauge her progress, Ray had stretched the tape measure around her navel each day when he got home. He'd weighed her, taken the calipers to her arms and ankles and breasts and kept the statistics in a logbook, then plotted the figures on graph paper. "And then there was shopping for the carriage."

Antoine was smiling now.

Lorraine saw that and felt easier. "Oh, God," she said. "Buying the carriage with Ray was like buying the Thunderbird. He read consumer reports, tested the wheels and the springs and the construction, *evaluated* the design. It had to be aerodynamically sound." She laughed, though at the time she'd liked Ray's enthusiasm. He wanted a family and nothing but the best would do.

Yet despite having taken care of her own mother, Lorraine had feared being a mother herself. Making the meals and doing the laundry were one thing — giving birth and dealing with an infant another. She needed advice, guidance. Ray had none, nor did he have a mother or sisters or aunts to step in. She had resorted to Dr. Spock's *Baby and Child Care* and had been immediately reassured by the subtitle of Chapter One: TRUST YOURSELF: you know more than you think you do. He encouraged her, he sounded like a nice man, the sort of man a grandfather should be. It was normal to feel blue — which she did — and she felt grateful at being allowed this.

When Ray saw the book he'd said, "What the hell kind of name is Spock?"

The most intriguing part of the book was Chapter 9: A father can now be an integral and essential part of the pregnancy and labour. There was even a line drawing showing a father wearing a medical gown holding the newborn, indicating he'd been there through the entire birth. She was allowed to ask Ray to accompany her into the terrifying world of the birthing room. She purposely left the book open so Ray would take the hint. He didn't. She was disappointed but also a little relieved. She wanted his support and encouragement, but was shy and fearful of the indignity of being seen sweaty and bloody and exposed.

The labour started on a Sunday afternoon in March and Ray drove her to the hospital. Again she wanted to ask him to come into the delivery room with her; even more, she wanted him to volunteer to be there, to insist on it. Instead, he withdrew as he always did during times of stress while she, scared, excited, said nothing. He escorted her through the pneumatic doors and up to the desk where he dealt with the nurse, signed something and Lorraine was put into a chair. After a peck on the cheek and a squeeze of the shoulder she was wheeled off along a green hallway past grisly iron machinery that looked more suited to a torture chamber than a maternity ward. Was this how her mother had felt when she'd been committed to the asylum? Was this how her dad had felt when he'd been drafted? You are now the property of Riverview Mental Hospital. You are now the property of the Royal Canadian Armed Forces. When Jack was born twelve hours later, Lorraine cried and wanted a hug. She hugged herself until a nurse returned with the baby and then Lorraine hugged him. *Embrasse-moi.*

One of the best things about having a child was being able to touch someone without the complications of sex. It was innocent and sensual at the same time. Lorraine loved the feel of her son's naked body next to hers, loved the smell of his head, the softness of his skin, the fineness of his hair and the perfection of his fingers. Everything about him from his toes to his lips to his saliva was perfect and pure.

"Everyone loves a child," said Antoine.

Lorraine smiled. "It changes you, yes."

"It changes everything."

Jack's birth had advanced Lorraine and Ray from a couple to a family. At last she'd escaped her mother and the hysterical insecurity of an abnormal adolescence. She was normal. She had proof, a son and a husband and a home. They received cards of congratulations and the neighbours dropped in. Dolly Gooch offered to show her the ropes at bingo, clubfoot Gene Rosencko stumped up the steps with a card of congratulations from his bedridden mother, Doreen Funt gave her a box of Darjeeling tea, Olivia Edson offered to babysit. People they'd only been on nodding terms with now stopped to chat. People visited with gifts and advice and tears in their eyes. Ray said she'd found her niche, and at the time Lorraine agreed. She was not just a married woman, but a mother. The bond between herself and her son was more profound than anything she'd ever imagined. She'd never known such satisfaction as when she breastfed him. She produced milk and he drank it. As for Ray, her enlarged breasts turned him on, which she liked, but between the two males she began to feel besieged. Eventually she worried she was disappearing, that her sole function was to feed her son and satisfy her man. The entire first year she was tired and absent-minded, her consciousness at risk of winking out like a candle flame.

But it blazed to life again when Ray sat her down one evening and laid out his plans for their future.

"See." He showed her various pages of graphs and tables.

"This is how we're going to work it. Five-year plans. Look. 1960 to 1965, 1965 to 1970, all the way to 2000."

Lorraine had watched his earnest face as he arranged the pages on the kitchen table. There it was, the rest of her life, down on paper. She looked at the headings and titles: Mortgage, Salary, Tax, Investments.

"The key is to establish a base." He looked at her to be sure she grasped the concept.

She nodded obediently.

"Like a building, it has to have a solid foundation." He pursed his lips and took a moment to contemplate the future. "We work hard, we focus, we can have that."

But what Lorraine was having was a panic attack, fear boring a hole in her heart. It felt as if she'd awakened on a train hours out of the station — the wrong train. She saw herself staring out the window at the rushing scenery. She saw herself staggering down the corridor from car to car past composed and confident faces.

"We can have that."

She'd looked at him. "Have what?"

He touched her wrist and leaned toward her, eager and patient and intent. "A life."

It was like an out-of-body experience. Lorraine saw for the first time what she'd done in marrying Ray — taken the wrong train.

Now Ray wanted her pregnant again. He wanted a daughter, he said. Didn't she want a daughter?

Well ...

Don't you?

Yet a voice inside her said no. Where did that voice come from? She knew that if she ignored that voice it would die, and if it died, so would she.

"*Je mourrais*," Lorraine told Antoine.

"But you had Jack." Antoine's white eyebrows were raised and his gaze cast downward. He'd been listening intently.

"What was your mother like?" Lorraine asked suddenly.

Caught off guard, Antoine didn't answer right away. "She had a stall in the market. Church items. Madonnas, prayer books, candles."

Lorraine thought of the enormous candles and saint statues for sale in the Saint Vincent de Paul store. They always made her feel solemn. Once she saw a nun there, an African woman in a long black robe with a white wimple framing her face. She was buying wine glasses.

"I was an altar boy," said Antoine, looking up at the evening sky. His tone of voice registered the absurdity of the fact.

"I'll bet you were a handsome altar boy."

He looked at her. "And you, you are Jewish?"

Lorraine saw the logic and was flattered to be taken for something other than what she was. "No. Just Ray. Though he's not really. He's nothing, an atheist."

Antoine considered that.

"I wanted to convert. He said no way. He got angry." She shrugged. "I went into a synagogue once. It was beautiful. I like churches, too. Old ones. It's like travelling. In Christ Church Cathedral there's all these plaques from World War I and II.

Memorials commemorating the dead."

"You think of your father."

"Yes." She felt Antoine watching her.

"The Greeks believed that immortality lay in being remembered."

⁂

"Ma'am. Are you all right?" asked the cop.

Lorraine stared at the tabletop and nodded.

"Is there anyone I can call? Your husband?"

"No. Yes. I mean, I'll call him." Lorraine went to the phone. The cop stood aside, lips compressed, eyebrows politely raised, looking, despite that broken nose, genuinely concerned about her. She was grateful. She dialled the number, finger fumbling twice in the hole so that she had to begin again, feeling, of all things, bad for the cop having to see her like this. When someone finally answered, she said, "Can I please speak to Mr. Klein?"

"Mr. Klein isn't here."

Lorraine didn't follow and she didn't recognize the voice. "Charlene?"

"Charlene's on vacation."

"And Mr. Klein —"

"Mr. Klein called in sick."

"Sick?"

"Is there a message?"

"No." Lorraine frowned. "No message." She hung up and saw both cops watching her.

"Problem, ma'am?" asked the older one.

Lorraine felt lightheaded and nauseous. Ray was sick? Had he pulled over and called from a booth? The clock on the stove read 9:55. He should be home by now. She'd maintained her composure in front of Jack, but now with the police here and this strange news about Ray she felt herself weakening.

"Ma'am?"

"He's ..." The room began to spin like a ferris wheel. She needed to sit down. She reached out. "He's on his way."

7
Spit Bugs

Recess passed and Jack was back in his seat. That hole in the desk was a snarling dog and the skin on his hand stung like it had been bitten. Mr. Gough had gripped Jack's wrist and twisted him free then sent him on his way.

Now Mr. Gough was chanting, "When two vowels go walking, the first one does the talking and says its own name."

For the next hour Jack sat very still and imitated the voices around him. When the lunch bell rang, Mr. Gough ordered them to eat at their desks. Jack snapped up the metal clasps of his Aladdin's lamp lunch box — bought new for school — and found a lettuce-and-tomato sandwich with mayonnaise wrapped in waxed paper, two plums from their tree, a McIntosh apple and a thermos of milk. Ivor didn't have a lunch box, he had a brown paper bag containing a wedge of rat cheese, the sort with the holes in it. He also had a stack of rye crisps, a jam jar of apple juice and a strip of pickled herring that stank of vinegar. Fat Boy Burton ate white bread sandwiches lined with shaved chocolate that he refused to trade. Miriam opened her Alice-in-Wonderland lunchbox and ate hard-boiled eggs. Mr. Gough paced the aisles between the desks monitoring them as they ate. At 12:20 he pointed to the row nearest the door.

"Up."

They stood up.

He pointed to the door. "This row. March."

The first thing Jack saw when he got outside was three Grade 7s kicking a boy on the ground. They kicked him and the boy laughed loudly as they did it. Then the boy on the ground got up and, still laughing, joined the others as they kicked a different kid. Jack kept his distance, wandering the fringes of the field watching the kids kicking, punching, piggybacking, spitting, burping and rolling in the dirt. Some of the Grade 7 boys almost had moustaches and sideburns and the girls had breasts.

Antoine's eyes had looked like melted wax. Jack wondered if that hurt.

A soccer ball rolled past. Instead of chasing it Jack merely watched it go by. Girls were playing skip, the rope slapping the asphalt as they chanted. Jack didn't understand skip. He felt sorry for girls having such useless games like skip and hop-scotch and dolls.

Gripping the chain-link fence, Jack remembered Steve McQueen trapped in barbed wire after the Germans had chased him down.

Jack found Ivor making kids pay for the thrill of breaking his toothpick-stiff hair. Each morning Ivor's mother combed his hair with Dabb, a cream that dried as hard as peanut brittle. Now Ivor stood behind the school collecting pennies, Dubble Bubbles, candy bananas, liquorice and marbles for the joy of snapping a stick of his lacquered red hair. Fat Boy Burton and Miriam stood back watching in disgust.

Sometimes Ivor drew lines connecting all his warts to see if they revealed a pattern, like the connect-the-dots in the newspaper. Jack's mom assured him warts were not caused by touching toads or frogs. He didn't fear snakes or cats or dogs, either. That's why he hadn't shrunk from the German shepherd last week when he and Ivor were playing right here behind the school. At the time — seven full days ago — starting Grade One seemed years away. He'd reached to pet the German shepherd, but instead of reacting like dogs usually did by licking his hand or wagging its tail, it locked its forelegs around Jack's knee and began to hump him. Jack didn't understand what the dog was doing but felt it was shameful, and he couldn't escape because the dog was big — bigger than him — and it growled and humped harder each time he tried pulling away. Its teeth were long and stained. Jack was starting to wail when Ivor pulled out Egbert's pellet pistol and began shooting.

The first shot skidded off the dirt. The next hit the dumpster and the lead pellet ricocheted off the metal side and nicked the wire-mesh over the nearest classroom window. Ivor fired two more pellets. One hit Jack in the crotch. The other hit the dog in the ear. The dog rocketed off like the Road Runner, leaving Jack on his back with his hands over his groin. That was how Mr. Fish, the janitor, had found him. Fish prodded Jack with the wet end of a mop. "Beat it."

Jack hobbled stiffly off across the field and up the alley and found Ivor hiding in Olivia Edson's garage. Jack pulled down his pants. His diddles was turning as black as a liquorice cigar and stung like it had been scorched. They were studying Jack's diddles when Egbert appeared wearing a grey sweatshirt inside out with the sleeves cut off. Damp red hair sprouted under his arms and he needed a shave on his chin and upper lip.

Egbert eyed them, suspicious gaze clicking from Ivor to Jack to Ivor. "Yer homos."

Jack didn't know what a homo was, but he knew enough to pull his zipper up.

Egbert kicked Ivor in the arse. "Kiss him."

"No!"

"Go on!"

"I already shot him," said Ivor, meaning that was even better. Jack knew Ivor had ways of deflecting Egbert, from playing the fool by turning his eyelids, to becoming Egbert's accomplice. Ivor had told Jack he wanted to be a Mountie when he grew up so he could ride a horse and arrest Egbert. Ivor showed Egbert the pellet pistol.

Seeing his own gun, Egbert grabbed it. "Whud I tell you?"

"You weren't using it!"

His voice got bigger. "Whud I tell you?"

"I got him a good one," said Ivor.

"Is there blood?"

"He's got a bruise."

"Where?"

Ivor pointed to Jack's crotch. "There!"

Egbert looked at Jack. "Did he?" Egbert's tone was ominous, warning him not to lie.

"Yeah!" Jack spoke enthusiastically, like it was great that Ivor had shot him.

"Let's see."

Jack reluctantly undid his zipper and pushed down his pants. Egbert leaned close and studied Jack's blackened and circumcised penis. Then he took a lighter from his pocket, snapped up a flame and swiped at Jack's penis as if to set it on fire. "Light yer nigger wick ya Jew prick."

Jack jumped back all the way to the garage wall and wrestled his zipper up. But Egbert had already forgotten him and turned his attention back to Ivor. Jack watched Egbert catch Ivor's wrist and give him an Indian burn, gripping his forearm with both hands and twisting opposite ways until Ivor yowled. Then Egbert held the lighter flame to Ivor's rear, but Ivor ran in circles and Egbert could only make the seat of his jeans smoke. After a minute of that, Egbert said, "Okay, okay," meaning it was safe now.

Ivor and Jack took turns with the lighter. It was a Dickson Drywall and Plaster lighter, yellow with black letters.

"Is that dad's?" asked Ivor.

"Duh."

Whenever Egbert or Ivor farted, Mr. Skog lit his lighter and waved it by their bum to burn away the smell.

They tried the lighter on their shoelaces and on the wood of the garage. Then Egbert discovered a patch of oil in the middle of the cement. Egbert said, "Fuck."

Jack and Ivor said, "Fuck." They stood at the edge of the oil like they'd discovered a secret lake.

"Ever hear a spider scream?"

Jack and Ivor shook their heads then watched Egbert trap a spider in the corner and return with it cupped in his hands and give them a look. "Ready?"

They nodded.

"Okay." Egbert shook the spider in his cupped hands, blew on them like a gambler seeking good luck, then tossed the spider onto the oil as if rolling dice. It hit and stuck. Three hairy legs were glued to the oil and the others waved like fingers. Jack thought of little Miss Muffet who sat on a tuffet, and he wondered what a tuffet was. The spider looked like it was drowning. Jack's dad said spider webs were miracles of nature, that a single strand of spider web was stronger than a single strand of steel. He said someday they'd build bridges of spider web.

"You hear it?"

Jack and Ivor listened, then shook their heads.

"No?"

Jack could see Egbert was enjoying himself. When Egbert was in a good mood it meant he wasn't dangerous and you could get near him. Once he made Loud Mouth Lime Kool-Aid, filling the jug three-quarters with sugar before adding the water, and they drank it straight from the jug. At those times Egbert intrigued Jack. Egbert once explained how if you couldn't spit in a guy's underpants then it was almost as good to spit in his socks.

"Listen again." Egbert snapped up a flame on his lighter and, smiling now, waved the lighter like a magician waving a wand and torched the oil. "Voila!" The fire flowed in a wave from one side of the oil to the other, right overtop of the spider. The flame floated there, yellow and blue, and Jack watched the smoke stream straight up to the rafters then curl back down. When they all began to cough they ran out of the garage right into Rat Gardecki and Olivia Edson.

"My garage!" shouted Olivia.

"Get a blanket!" shouted Rat.

As Olivia dashed back into the house, Egbert dodged left then right but Rat dropped into a wrestler's crouch and collared him. When Egbert pulled out the pellet pistol Rat flipped him with a judo throw, grabbed the pistol and knelt on Egbert's head. Egbert cried out and his arms and legs writhed like snakes. Olivia returned with a beige blanket. She'd lost one of her shoes and limped over the gravel, her piled hair collapsed and dangling over her ear. She threw the blanket over Egbert.

Rat shut his eyes and then, very calmly, very quietly said, "The fire. Not him. The fire."

"God!" She hauled the blanket off Egbert and threw it over the oil, but by then the flames had died.

Rat looked at Jack with an expression that said he was

disappointed in him. "What the hell you doin' hangin' around with this bone brain?"

Jack just stood there. Ivor put his hands up like they did on *Gunsmoke*.

That evening Rat and Olivia came over and there was a conference in the kitchen. Jack listened at his bedroom door.

"Kid's a pyro," said Rat.

"You laying charges?" Jack's dad asked.

"Well, I nearly had a heart attack," said Olivia. "One minute we're drinking tea and the next there's smoke pouring from the garage! It's that father of theirs."

"What about that retard daughter?" said Rat. "Always wandering around down in the bush by the lake."

"If she was my daughter I wouldn't let her go down there alone," said Ray. Jack knew there were stories of hobos living in the bush around Rain Lake. When Jack thought of hobos he thought of Freddy-the-Freeloader on *The Red Skelton Hour*. His dad told him to stay away from Rain Lake, but he and Ivor went anyway.

"She brings her father his lunch," said Lorraine. "He works in that drywall plant. It gives her something to do."

"Something to do? I know what I'd like to do with *him*," said Rat.

Jack heard a slapping sound and knew Rat was punching his palm. Rat always punched his palm to make a point.

They began discussing the Skogs.

"Eva still conditions her hair with mayonnaise," said Olivia.

"I used to use mayonnaise," said Lorraine.

Jack's dad was appalled. "When?"

"When I was a teenager. It was all we could afford."

Jack imagined his mom putting mayonnaise in her hair. He remembered Ivor dunking celery into mayonnaise.

"Did I tell you what Skog did?" asked Rat. "Comes in for gas last week and paid in pennies. Counted out a hundred and seventy goddamn cents. You believe it? Pennies! Didn't even have them rolled up. Gum and dirt and who knows what all over them. Time before that he tried paying in beer bottles!"

"Get out of here," said Ray.

"I'm tellin' ya. Had a trunk full of 'em. I said this isn't a bloody bottle depot, fella. He says whataya mean, it's money. I said, you want gas you bring proper currency. I'm not trottin' your bottles down to the liquor store."

Jack heard the adults laugh, not ha ha laughs, but disgusted laughs.

"Have you talked to him about Egbert's little garage stunt?" asked Ray.

"Goddamn right I have. Guess what the bugger said? *Boys will be boys.* I said boys may be boys, but that kid's an animal. Belongs in a cage. Pulls another number like that I'll kick his arse around the block, believe you me."

Jack continued watching the kids pay to snap sticks of Ivor Skog's hair. Jack didn't want to snap Ivor's hair, he wanted to tell Ivor about Antoine and the birds. He wanted Ivor to get Egbert to do something to Mr. Gough. "Ivor. Ivor ..." But Ivor was too busy, so Jack kicked at the dirt and wandered along to where the fence had unravelled. In the bush across the street small birds flitted in the trees and Jack thought of the canaries. Maybe he'd have to get a butterfly net and climb the plum tree to catch them. He wished Antoine would marry Grandma Estelle and be his grandfather. He wished his dad didn't get mad every time Antoine was mentioned. When he asked his dad why he didn't like Antoine, he said he didn't dislike Antoine, but Jack knew that was a fib. A fib wasn't as bad as a lie, just like swiping wasn't as bad as stealing.

Jack tugged at the unravelled fence and realized he could escape. His heart thumped against his chest. He looked back at the school where Mr. Gough was waiting with his yardstick. Jack ducked through the hole in the fence and stood in the weedy grass on the other side. It felt different over here. He felt fear and relief and was breathing fast. He wasn't supposed to be outside the fence. Steve McQueen wasn't even supposed to be near the fence in *The Great Escape*. He stood very still waiting for someone to yell at him, but no one did, no one was even watching. Those Grade 7s were kicking a different boy now and kids were still eager to snap sticks of Ivor's hair. Jack quietly crossed the street that had bottle caps embedded in the tar and waded into the high fragrant grass, avoiding the spit bugs. Soon he was hidden amid the trees and smelled sap and wood. If he kept going he'd hit Rain Lake where, in the tea-coloured water, there was said to be a car with a skeleton. All summer Jack and Ivor had poled a raft around the lake but hadn't found it. Ivor said the skeleton might have gold teeth they could pry out and sell.

Jack moved deeper into the familiar bush and it was as if the trees were welcoming him back, brushing him with their branches, patting his shoulders, *Hello. Hello. Welcome home. Where have you been?* Twigs cracked under his step and wind pushed through the leaves making the sound of applause. Everything was green and gold like sunshine on treasure. He heard crows and gulls and the *chickadee-dee-dee* of birds whose name he didn't know. Then he heard the crows begin cawing louder as if in warning and Jack thought they were warning each other about him until he spotted a scruffy white cat with a pigeon flapping in its mouth. Jack threw a stick and the cat crouched. He threw another stick and then another and the cat dropped the bird and darted up a tree.

When Jack picked up the pigeon, its head lolled and he thought of the *feznt* in the picture by the kitchen table. The pigeon was alive, though, sleek and warm and trembling in his hands. It had white and grey feathers and watched him. Jack heard the school bell ring in the distance. He crouched. He wasn't going back to school. He'd live here in the bush and when the pigeon was better it would be grateful and carry messages to Ivor and Antoine and maybe his mother, but only if she promised not to make him go back to school where the dog had humped him and Mr. Gough had squeezed his head.

When the bell stopped ringing and it was quiet again, Jack pushed his way deeper into the bush, pausing to eat blackberries and salal berries — offering them to the bird, which showed no desire to eat. He wished he'd brought his lunch box and that a real genie lived in his Aladdin's lamp thermos, a genie with a sword and an earring and three wishes to give him. If he had three wishes he'd wish Antoine was better, that he didn't have to go to school, and that he was a genie himself. If he was a genie he'd never have to worry about Egbert Skog.

He reached the lake and looked for the raft. He spotted something else, something new, something unexpected, something he didn't understand. In the long and boggy grass beneath a blue sky Ivor's dad — pants down — was kneeling behind Ivor's sister Nadia who was on all fours with her dress pushed up. A lunch box was open and there were beer bottles and a metal thermos. Mr. Skog and Nadia made noises and they looked busy. Jack knew not to interrupt when adults were busy, even if one of them was not really an adult but Nadia. Mr. Skog's bony bum moved back and forth, back and forth, and he was making noises: hoo, hoo, hoo. Nadia's bum was big and round and jiggled. Mr. Skog reached around and squeezed her boob. Then Mr. Skog's bum began going faster and so did his noises: hoo!hoo!hoo! On her hands and knees, Nadia stretched out her tongue — a long red wet tongue — and slid it up her nose. That's when Jack gasped and Mr. Skog spotted him. The face he made caused Jack to drop the pigeon and sprint through the trees that whipped his face with their branches as if to punish him.

❖

The first time Jack had seen Nadia she was petting bees. He thought she was beautiful. It was just a few days after meeting Ivor and she was standing close to the vines running up the side of house, whispering to the bees and petting them. Jack thought she was picking the orange berries his dad warned him were poisonous, but she wasn't, she was stroking the big black-and-yellow bumblebees. She caressed their furred backs as if they were cats, and they didn't mind, they didn't even seem to notice, they just continued buzzing from flower to flower. Nadia had red hair like Ivor but it was straight and smooth and shiny and her face was full and fat like a baby's. To Jack, Nadia seemed as serene as a flower. When she discovered Jack watching her she smiled and without a word wrapped him up in a hug that felt soft and smelled of soap.

"My name's Nadia and I'm sweet sixteen peaches and cream."

Then she showed him how to pet bees, taking his hand in hers and guiding his finger. He spent the afternoon with Nadia, talking only in whispers and touching the finely downed bees and watching them work. Until then, all Jack knew was that bees were like wasps and hornets and yellow jackets, and they all stung.

When Jack told Ivor about petting bees, Ivor frowned. When he told his mother she said be careful. When he told Antoine he said in Japan they keep crickets as pets. When he told his father he said Nadia Skog was a mongoloid.

Jack didn't understand. "A mango Lloyd?"

"A retard," explained his dad, "like the people where your grandmother lives." Jack felt tricked, he felt foolish, like the time he found a chunk of chalk on the grass and his dad laughed and pointed and said it was poo, sun-bleached poo, and Jack realized that it was.

Jack burst from the bush oblivious to the white foam of the spit bugs streaking his new pants and shirt. He crossed the street without looking both ways, ducked through the hole in the chain-link fence and trotted on across the empty schoolyard toward the stone steps that stood as steep and dark as the steps of a castle. Somehow Jack knew that what Mr. Skog and Nadia were doing was like the German shepherd humping him.

All the classroom doors were closed. He searched the hall for room 102. From one room came chanting: *Five times five is twenty-five* ... He was having trouble breathing, like the time he fell out of the plum tree and landed on his back. The doors were vast and green with big round copper knobs. He wandered the hall until he spotted an open door, smaller than the others and with no numbers above it. Outside the door he saw a mop standing in a bucket. As he got near he saw it was not a room but a closet and yet there was a man in it, Mr. Fish, the janitor who'd poked him with the mop. From five feet away Jack smelled the onions burning in his armpits. Mr. Fish looked like a troll from one of Jack's picture books: dark, lean and unshaven, hair sprouting like ditch-grass from his collar. He wore a green shirt and green pants. But he wasn't like Mr. Greenjeans. Mr. Fish was squeezing the water from a mop and talking to it. He stuck the mop's head into a kind of vise in a bucket and pressed the handle down hard so water gushed out the holes and he whispered the way Egbert Skog had whispered that he wanted to see Antoine's canaries, but Mr. Fish said — as if talking into the mop's ear — "How's your headache now, you bitch? How's your headache now?"

Eventually Jack found a door that felt familiar, a door with numbers near the top. 102. He put his ear to the wood and was relieved to hear Mr. Gough's voice come through muted but distinct. Jack gripped the doorknob with both hands and turned it.

"Numbers! Who can tell me the name of the first number? Who can —"

Jack watched Mr. Gough turn and look at him. The class looked at him too, with fearful faces, but Mr. Gough looked at him with a wide smile showing all his teeth, beaver teeth. Jack imagined Mr. Gough on his hands and knees in the forest, still wearing his shoes and suit, chewing at a tree trunk. Mr. Gough began to laugh. He let his head drop back and he laughed and he laughed so that great clouds of laugh-smoke pumped from his mouth. Jack was relieved at making the right decision in returning to school, that all of a sudden Mr. Gough had become what his dad said was an "easygoing guy," like Rat Gardecki, like Dean Martin on TV, who was also an easygoing guy. Then Mr. Gough's head snapped forward and he was not laughing.

Mr. Gough's expression drove Jack back until he bumped against the door behind him and the cold hard knob pressed like a fist against his spine.

"Well, well, well. Jack is late again. Not once, but twice. Two times on his first day of school." Jack watched Mr. Gough consider him. "That's a bit of a record, I think. Yes, I'd say we have a record holder here." Mr. Gough looked at the class, inviting them to share his wonder. "Tell us, Jack. Why are you late?"

Jack didn't dare mention Mr. Skog and Nadia.

"Did you forget the classroom number?"

"No."

"No, what?"

"No, sir."

"What is the classroom number?"

Jack forgot.

"You can't remember, but you found your way." Mr. Gough looked to the class again. "Little lost Jack found his way back." He smiled. The kids giggled. Mr. Gough slammed his desk causing everyone to jump. He pointed to a stool in a corner at the front of the room. "Sit."

8

We Are the Engineers!

Ray passed the Sun Tower, once the tallest building in the British Commonwealth. Off to his right was the huge neon W on top of Woodward's Department Store. One year, as their annual prank, the U.B.C. Engineers had planned to steal that W but were warned by a law student that Chunky Woodward — the owner — would sue them, *Three ways from Thursday.*

That had been one of many subjects discussed last Saturday night at Ray's ten-year U.B.C. reunion. Lon Wells and Croft Stickard had been there. They were three years younger than Ray — who'd done two years in the army and one in a sawmill — and now they were Wells & Stickard Chemical Engineering of Toronto, big movers and shakers in plastics. When Ray had returned from Europe, guys like Wells and Stickard didn't want to hear about the war. For years they'd been hearing about how grateful they should be, how a sacrifice had been made and how they'd committed the crime of being born too late to pitch in. So even though he'd missed the real action himself, a guy like Ray Klein pissed off Lon Wells and Croft Stickard.

That's why two things Ray saw at the reunion made him happy: Lon was bald, and Croft had so much blubber he needed a bra.

Lon said, "What're you driving, Ray?"

"T-bird. You?"

Lon's smile staggered. "Caddie."

Ray asked Lon if he was married.

"No way."

Ray smiled. "Still on manual, eh."

Lon gave him a shot on the shoulder — a hard shot.

What really burned Ray about Wells and Stickard was that his army training didn't scare either of them. Ray was five-ten and weighed one-eighty, yet here was Lon giving him one in the shoulder.

"I hear you're in Selwyn's stable," said Croft.

"What're you doing?" smirked Lon. "Designing sawdust piles?"

Ray laughed to gain a moment to work up a withering comeback, but he couldn't. He was better with numbers than words. He described Selwyn's current contract, designing a system of automated scissor-lift lumber stackers for a small plywood mill in south Vancouver. Wells and Stickard both made a show of yawning and checking their Rolexes. Ray-boy's time was up. After that Ray avoided them for the rest of the reunion, though he kept his ears alert in case they were talking about him.

The do had taken place in a suite at the Sylvia Hotel in the West End, right across the street from English Bay and not far from Charlene's apartment. Down there in the water, swimmers backstroked across a setting sun. A gold-dust light filled the hotel room and glinted off cufflinks and tie pins and rings and gold-capped teeth. Ray overheard Lon going on about Broadway Joe Namath.

"Bugger's getting four hundred thousand for signing with the Jets. Four hundred thou and he's never thrown a pass! Average player makes ten."

"Guy should be cleaning toilets," said Croft.

"Speaking of toilets," said Lon. "Denise Daniels."

Ray watched them snort and elbow and wink.

Lon put his hand to his mouth and shouted like a carnival barker, "Come one, come all!"

"Married that ricer," said Croft. "What was his name, Wong, Fong, Dong?"

Ray didn't remember any Denise Daniels, though he did recall Gary Tong, who hadn't bothered showing.

Whoever organized the reunion not only pinned class pictures to the walls, but *Playboy* centrefolds and a recent photo interview with Hugh Hefner in *Chatelaine*. Ray looked at the article with interest. There was Hef lounging amid his toys in his Chicago pad, pipe in his mouth, pronouncing upon sex. There was Hef lounging on his round, eight-and-a-half-foot diameter revolving bed. There was Hef in his maroon smoking jacket with black satin cuffs and lapels. *Playboy* made a twenty million dollar profit in 1964, said Hef. And there was a shot of Hef by the pool, stating that women should do more with their lives than raise kids. Frank and Dino and Sammy and Peter Lawford had all romped in the Playboy mansion with Hef. They were living the life, and the article said men around the world could only envy them. Yet Ray didn't envy them. Sure, he admired the rollicking roguishness of the Rat Pack, but Hugh Hefner was a pimp. Taking in the manly chortling around him, Ray wondered: what was Hef's great contribution? A bridge? An aqueduct? Penicillin? No. A masturbation aid. Well, so was a sock.

Ray thought of his own contribution, then thought of Lorraine and Jack. He missed them with such sudden intensity he almost ducked into the bathroom to hide in case someone saw his tears. Ray stood close to the window and looked out beyond the maple trees at the sea and the freighters and the horizon. He felt like a shit for playing around on Lorraine. He thought of how she'd look if she found out, the way her eyes would fill with tears. Behind him ice clinked in glasses and beer bottles hissed as the caps were popped. The room smelled of cigarettes and cologne, armpits and beer. A sorry get-together all around, he concluded. Maybe he shouldn't have come? Maybe he wasn't supposed to have come? The realization stabbed him. Was that why Wells and Stickard were being such shits?

Anti-Semitism still caught him off guard. And it happened at the oddest times, like when he'd decided to take up golf.

First he'd practised in his living room with a mop handle, trying the various grips and swings recommended in *Danny Dean's Tips for Tee Off.* When he had the theory down he bought clubs and went to the driving range. He set his feet, gripped the club, executed a slow back swing and — eyes never leaving the ball — followed smoothly through. But again and again he'd fan the ball entirely, succeeding only in wrenching his back and embarrassing himself. If he did connect he hooked or sliced or topped it. Sometimes he hit the ground itself, the jolt reverberating up the club into his elbows. He kept at it though because Dino golfed. They played golf all year round in Vegas. Golf meant leisure and money and acceptance. Jack Nicklaus and Arnie Palmer and Gary Player were all tanned and relaxed and in control. They strolled the fairways with the sun glinting off their clubs. No one sweated or grunted or tackled or kicked or slashed much less cross-checked you into the boards. Golfers had all their teeth. He imagined rambling about the greens with the guys, jawing about this or that, a tee behind the ear, and afterwards hitting the nineteenth hole for a rye and seven. All one summer he practised on his own. At work, Ray listened to the golf talk, nodding and smiling and putting his two bits in like he knew all about it — eagle, birdie, double bogie — but never once did they ask him if he was interested in making up a foursome. At first he didn't understand, then it hit him. He sold the clubs.

Croft Stickard belched and announced, "Hey, it's chemical engineering or nothing. You wanna lay sewer lines — fine. Be a dickhead."

"Fusion reactors," said a guy Ray didn't remember.

"Fuck fusion," said another, "*fission* reactors."

Talk drifted to the military and Rex Cedric who'd gone to the U.S. and was in tank design. Rex had been too busy to make the reunion, which added to his status. They compared the British Chieftain, the American M-60 — which had a 105-mm gun and 750 hp diesel engine — and the Russian PT-76, which was amphibious.

Ray knew the Swedes had just come out with a turretless tank called the Bofors — but didn't bother mentioning it. He merely watched the hotshots do the cock walk. To hell with them. He had a career, a wife, a kid, a T-Bird, and a mistress who was centrefold material. Pretty soon he'd have a bigger house, maybe another kid, too. Lon Wells and Croft Stickard were old money Shaughnessy boys. Ray's mother had cleaned houses in Shaughnessy. He remembered how she'd taped felt insoles to her knees when she scrubbed floors. Along with her hourly wage, she had brought home cast-off clothing, furniture, broken utensils, the heel ends of bread loaves, bruised fruit, turkey bones. She never let food go to waste. It wasn't just that they were poor, but that it was free. His mother felt obliged to eat free food even if she hated it, because free food was good food no matter what. The same principle held with clothes. Like it or not, Ray appeared at school in oddly matched shirts and trousers twenty and thirty years out of date, and as a result was dubbed Ray Clown. He argued with his mother.

"I look like a hobo!"

"That's Shetland wool!"

He stashed vests and smoking jackets under the porch on his way out and put them on again when he got home. Shoes proved more difficult. Though it was the height of the Depression, for health reasons the school enforced a no bare-foot policy and so for weeks Ray went to class in soccer boots; it was that or Persian slippers. His mother was ingenious. She struggled mightily with the challenge of transforming shirt-sleeves into pant legs and Ray had no choice but to wear them.

Ray grew up in a house he nicknamed "the coffin," a two-room saltbox off Commercial Drive, Vancouver's Little Italy, where in the thirties if you were lucky enough to work at all you worked on the waterfront or in the mills. His dad spent his time at the kitchen table fiddling with clocks and watches, in the padded chair with the carved oak arms by the Marconi, or in the wicker chair on the porch. No matter where he was he wore the same haunted expression, a look of preoccupation, as if he'd stop breathing if he didn't concentrate. Then one night in December 1939, he did stop breathing. He was forty-four. Ray's twelve-year-old brother Del died of rheumatic fever in 1945 — a look of betrayal in his young eyes, outraged at being knocked out of the game so soon — and then that winter his mother died of Asian flu.

The place was a rental, owned by a Calabresi named Santelli whose clan of women came in to help deal with the clothes and furniture and utensils. They arrived wearing black, even the daughter who was Ray's age. Feeling abandoned, Ray went through the closet and drawers in his parents' room seeking some sign, a note or a message to guide him on through the rest of his life.

Alone at eighteen, Ray joined the army.

⁂

Ray hit the liquor store just as it opened. He liked liquor stores for their shelves of sleek and elegant bottles. The fact that the limits of industrial glass production determined the design of the bottles didn't detract from his appreciation, perhaps even enhanced it. He especially liked the frosting on the Gilbey's gin bottle. He got the rye, then crossed to Zeller's. The clerks here were all high-haired matrons. He bought an Arrow shirt and a box of Kleenex, then stepped outside and found a pay phone. He discovered a dime waiting in the slot as if someone had set it there just for him, and decided it was his day after all.

Heading back to the car, he passed a deli called Klein's Kosher Meats, the name painted in bold black letters. He looked through the window. He'd never seen the place before. He watched an aproned man behind the counter run a salami back and forth across a slicer. Klein. Was it possible Ray and the man were related? Could he be a cousin, a second cousin? How common a name was Klein? The man was too old to be a cousin but something about him looked familiar, something in the bend of the back and the way he used his hands, something Old World. The man reminded him of his father's uncle, an old man who'd been sitting on the good chair at the kitchen table when Ray came home from school one afternoon.

Ray was ten and in the fifth grade at the time. He heard the arguing and the strange voice even before he opened the door. When he entered, his mother and father and the stranger fell silent and turned to him. The stranger smiled and made a big nodding gesture of welcome. Ray had looked from his mother to his father, but they suddenly seemed different — different in the way Ugo Andretti changed when he switched from English to Italian.

"So," said the visitor in an accent that sounded simultaneously friendly and suspicious, "here he is. At last we meet."

That scared Ray. It meant he'd been discussed, as if plans were forming behind his back and his life was about to take some turn.

"This is Avram," said his mother. "Your father's uncle." His mother, who was holding three-year-old Del in her lap, added, "Uncle Avram's from Montreal."

Avram wore a dark suit, had an olive complexion, a long granite-coloured beard and was bald on top. His hat sat on the table.

"How was school?"

"Okay." Avram? And even as Ray wondered, he understood that this was a Jewish name.

"He's a good student," put in his mother.

Avram nodded, pleased and impressed. "What are you studying?" He narrowed his eyes and raised his chin awaiting the response.

Ray shrugged. "Germany."

"Germany." Avram nodded again as if to say that was an

important subject. "Raymond." He sat forward and gazed intently. "Raymond, tell me, do you know who you are?"

"For Christ's sake!" said Ray's father.

Without shifting his gaze, Avram raised a hand for silence and to Ray's amazement his dad obeyed.

Ray knew what Avram meant. He was a Jew. Ray had seen the articles in the paper about Hitler and National Socialism, he'd seen the newsreels before the Bowery Boys movies on Saturday afternoon that showed masses of marching Germans shouting their Roman legion chant of *Seig Heil*! He'd heard the word Jew spat at his feet even as he delivered newspapers. Why, he wondered, did no one ever say anything to Gordon Cline who was in the same class? How did they know Klein from Cline?

Ray understood that in Vancouver you had to be careful. If you were Chinese, Japanese, Italian, Slavic, or a Jew, it meant you were an outsider, and all kinds of doors were closed. Not wanting to stick out, the Kleins celebrated Christmas and ignored Hanukkah. That was fine with Ray. He shrugged. "I dunno. Me."

Avram smiled patiently. "You. Of course you're you. But you're — "

"Avram!"

"A Jew. Do you know what that means?"

"It means nothing!" said his father.

Voice high and resonant with conviction, Avram said, "It means a great deal. Otherwise why deny it? Otherwise why run out here to —" his hand rose and he struggled for the word as if he'd forgotten where he was "— *British* Columbia? The end of the world."

Enraged, Ray's father rose wheezing from his chair. Avram calmly faced him. Ray's mother put an arm around her husband and they stood frozen until Ray broke the tableau by saying quietly, "I got homework." He went into the bedroom and sat with his fists clenched between his knees.

❖

Mind still stuck in his memories, Ray let the traffic entangle him on West Georgia. Within seconds the other cars had bricked him in on all sides. Opposite the courthouse a mob waving placards strained and swelled around the fountain and up the steps to the pillared portico. There were cops all over. "What the ..." he called across to a Chinese guy in a postal van. "What the hell's goin' on?"

"That Nazi."

"Who?"

"The guy. In the news. Schell."

Ray squinted to read the placards but was too far away. What he could see was the long hair. First it was beatniks, now it was hippies. But there was a difference. Hippies were political. "Shit." He was getting screwed out of his poke with Charlene by some hippies, and he was sweating up his new shirt. He spotted the rye in its paper bag. He wanted a swig. He wanted Charlene. He switched on the radio and punched buttons hunting news, but there was only a burst of the Beatles, a jabbering DJ, the weather report: *81 degrees and not a cloud in the sky.*

9
Funeral Arrangements

Lorraine sat at the kitchen table with a cold cloth across her forehead. The cop had caught her when she'd staggered and had guided her to the chair. Even as the vertigo had whirled through her, a distant voice she recognized as her own was already apologizing. "Oh dear, I'm sorry, I'm ..." The Formica felt cool under her forearms. She wanted to shut her eyes and lay her cheek on the tabletop, but thought it unseemly with the police here, as embarrassing for them as for her.

"The undertaker'll be here soon," said the older cop.

His voice was so soothing Lorraine knew he must have kids — daughters — and was used to coping with crisis. He had brown eyes and fleshy ears. The word undertaker lodged in her brain like a bone in the throat. She managed to turn to him, wanting to argue, wanting to say they'd made a mistake, that there was no need for an undertaker here, what they wanted was an ambulance. She tried to speak but nothing came out.

"Ma'am?"

Lorraine felt paralyzed.

The cop refreshed the cloth for her.

It was all too much. Antoine dead and now Ray, where was Ray? She pressed the cloth to her face with trembling hands and held it there, hiding behind it. Ray should be home by now, unless he went to the doctor, unless something else happened ...

"Nice globe," said the younger cop.

Lorraine lifted her face from the cloth and looked at the cop standing by the globe in the living room by the TV.

Antoine had given it to her, a wonderfully detailed leather-covered globe. It was as wide as one of the Thunderbird's wheels and filled an entire corner of the living room. Lorraine loved it. Jack loved it. Ray was suspicious. He'd stood in front of it with his fists on his hips as outraged as if it was a see-through negligee Antoine had given her.

"What's he doing giving you a globe?"

Lorraine lied. "It's for Jack."

"Jack?" Ray looked at Jack as if being introduced to him for the first time. "Is it?"

Lorraine heard the threat in his voice. "Jesus, Ray, he's six."

"You like the globe, Jack?"

"Who doesn't like a globe, Ray? Except you, that is."

Jack had told Lorraine it smelled like polished shoes. "It smells like shoes," he said now.

Ray gave it a suspicious sniff. "He's right. It stinks."

"It's good," said Jack.

"It's educational," said Lorraine. As if to demonstrate, she pointed to the bottom of the globe. "Look, Jack. Tierra del Fuego. That means the land of fire." She pointed to a spot near the top. "That's Iceland. And here's Arabia, where Aladdin lived with his magic lamp. Aladdin. Like your lunch box. And there's the ocean."

Lorraine watched Jack look at the ocean. She knew he was especially intrigued by the medieval-looking sea monster depicted with claws and fangs and whiskers swimming in the South Atlantic.

"That's the world," said Lorraine. "The earth. Where we live."

Ray wasn't convinced. He knew that Antoine was up to something. "Okay, Jacko." Ray tugged the knees of his trousers and squatted before him. "What've you learned? Come on. Tell us what wonderful things you've learned from this globe."

"Ray —"

He held up his hand cutting her off. "Come on, buddy. Whataya know?"

Lorraine listened to Ray's tone of voice — urging and playful and yet serious all at the same time — and watched it make Jack's eyes waver with worry. She knew he was wondering what his dad wanted to hear.

"Madagascar."

"Mada — *what*?"

"Madagascar."

Ray looked at Lorraine and she saw he was feeling excluded and suspicious.

"See."

"See what?"

Lorraine said, "Where's Madagascar, Jack?"

Jack went to the globe and pointed to the long island off the southeast coast of Africa.

"Big deal."

But Lorraine saw she'd won.

On rainy days Lorraine and Jack played spin the globe. They sat on the floor taking turns shutting their eyes and giving the globe a twirl. When it stopped they reached out and touched it with a fingertip, then opened their eyes to see what country they'd visit. This was the way Jack learned to read. That was how he'd learned about Madagascar, that first day the globe was installed in the living room. He'd sounded out the words slowly, syllable by syllable, under Lorraine's guidance. "Ma ... da ... gas ... car."

"What will we see when we get to Madagascar?" asked Lorraine.

Jack thought about that. Then it came to him. "The cars on Mad-a-gas-car are crazy."

Lorraine always enjoyed this part. "Why?"

"Because they put *mad gas* in them."

Lorraine applauded. There was no doubt, he was a spirit, a creature. The very thought of him ever being hurt made her entire body spasm in pain. "My turn." She closed her eyes and spun the globe. When it stopped she touched it.

"You always touch France." And it was true. Without even trying her finger always found France.

Lorraine shrugged and pointed. "Can you read that?"

It took Jack a while, but with his mother's help he sounded it out. "Lor-raine ..." Jack looked at his mother. "That's you."

"C'est moi," she said.

"Say mwa," said Jack.

Lorraine kissed him. *"Mwa!"* Then she cupped his face in her hands and looked at him. "Would you like to go to France, Jack?"

He gazed up at her.

It hurt her to see doubt and worry in his eyes.

He nodded.

What did he fear, she wondered, that she'd go off without him and his dad?

⌗

The cop went to the sink and ran Lorraine a glass of water. Then he sat down opposite her at the table and opened his notebook. "I know this is awkward."

Lorraine stared at Joe Kapp, the B.C. Lions' quarterback, on the water glass. Ray had got two of them at Rat's gas station with a fill-up. He'd got wine glasses, water glasses and once a case of Tab. She tried sipping some of the water but her hand trembled and it slopped.

The cop proceeded with business as delicately as he could. "Did he seem depressed?"

"Do you have kids?"

His fleshy forehead creased like soft leather as he raised his eyebrows and studied her. "Two girls."

Did they feel protected? Did they fear him? What an awful life, she thought, to be a cop. "Girls. That's nice."

"Was he depressed?"

"No. I don't know. I don't think so."

"Nothing was bothering him?"

Lorraine tried to think. Her face was sticky with tears and her nose plugged. "Excuse me." She went into the bathroom and got some toilet paper, blew her nose and washed her face with cold water. She saw Ray's razor. Every morning he managed to cut himself. Jack loved watching him shave and Ray sometimes chased him, threatening to shave him bald as a fish. She imagined Ray's relief upon learning Antoine was dead. The lines would leave his face as if a wind had blown them away. Where was Ray? What was he up to, calling in sick?

When she returned to the kitchen, the cop, smelling of uniform and boot polish and sweat, did his best to smile sympathetically. "How was his health?"

"He walked every day." Antoine was lean — even a little gaunt about the eyes — but his colouring was always pink.

"I noticed a vodka bottle."

"Mostly he drank wine."

The cop made a note. "A lot of wine?"

"He was French."

The cop's cranberry cheeks suggested he drank a bit himself. Lorraine figured she'd drink too if she was a cop. There were women cops in England. She'd read about it. She'd never want to be a cop. She imagined a life of metal and rage.

"Was he on any medication?"

"No."

"Under psychiatric care?"

"No."

"You're certain?"

Lorraine's eyes blinked. "I ... no."

"You're not certain."

"I guess not."

"Family?"

"Maybe. In France."

"Friends?"

Lorraine had never seen any, another thing that had always made Ray suspicious. "I don't know. I mean, me."

"You were close?

Lorraine thought about the picture. "Well."

The cop didn't press the issue. "What did he do for a living?" Lorraine didn't want to say she didn't know again. What *had* he done? He rarely talked about himself. Only now did Lorraine realize just how little she knew. She recalled something about teaching in Algeria, operating a radio on a merchant ship, cooking in a logging camp up north. He seemed to have done everything but she knew nothing about it. "He was retired."

The cop probed his ear with his pen. "Anything else you can tell us? Anything at all?"

"He had nightmares."

The cop wrote. "What about?"

"He never said. But I'd hear him." The cop made another note.

His handwriting slanted like grass in a wind. The pen was like a toothpick in his fingers. Lorraine imagined his girls holding his hands, one on either side of him as they walked. She imagined him carrying them one on each hip. "How old are they?"

"Excuse me?"

"Your daughters."

He watched her. "Nineteen and twenty."

"What do they do?"

"One's starting university and one's in Europe. France."

Lorraine stared at his brown eyes and heard his kind voice: a father, a man who coped well with crisis, not handsome, but attractive. She wondered what his name was. "Were you in the war?"

The cop glanced at his partner, but the younger man merely raised his eyebrows in an expression of innocence. "Yes, I was."

"My father died at Dieppe."

He cleared his throat. "I'm sorry." He waited what he deemed a suitable length of time before continuing. "So, Mr. Gah-din."

"Go-dan."

"Go-dan. He had nightmares."

"Yes." Lorraine described how two or three times a week Antoine woke shouting. Lorraine always heard because she slept badly herself. The one time she mentioned them he claimed not to remember, but did admit to insomnia. He'd smiled and said he'd become a connoisseur of the night. Lorraine liked that, even though she could see he was covering up. She said she too had trouble sleeping. She said she'd get up and sit by the window, just listening, or switch the radio to FM and find a jazz station from Seattle or San Francisco. Every time Ray found her awake he said take sleeping pills or valerian tea. Lorraine felt sad for him because he was missing the romance of the night. She discovered that when she spoke to Antoine about her insomnia he became more interested in her, looking into the depths of her eyes. Encouraged, she exaggerated her condition and a half hour's sleeplessness became an entire night and then an entire lifetime. She felt guilty, but did it anyway.

"When did you see him last?" asked the cop.

"Saturday evening."

They'd sat on a blanket on the lawn beneath the plum tree drinking wine. The door to Antoine's suite had been open and from the hi-fi came Edith Piaf singing "Amour." As they talked, a plum thudded the blanket by Antoine's hand. He picked it up and without taking his eyes from Lorraine, said, "*Merci*, Jack."

"Want one, Mom?"

"I've had three, thanks. And you've had enough, too. You'll be on the pot all night."

Jack lay stretched out along the branch right above their heads. It was his branch and so perfectly shaped he could fall asleep up there, something Lorraine envied and admired. Who but a cat or a kid could sleep in a tree? She knew he was watching them. "It looks like checkers," he'd said at one point and Lorraine understood he meant the way they shifted things, a glass, a napkin, a plate, on the checked blanket.

Lorraine had been pressing Antoine about his travels and Antoine, reluctantly at first, enigmatic as always, told her he'd once walked from Athens to Istanbul.

"Istanbul." Lorraine savoured the word and all it conjured: the Orient Express, Islam, intrigue, spies.

"And then I sailed to Trebizond."

"Trebizond." Lorraine thought of Trebizond tucked away in the far corner of the Black Sea.

"Herodotus wrote of the mad honey of Trebizond."

Lorraine grew wary, suspecting he was putting her on. "Mad honey?"

"Xerxes' army returning from defeating the Persians ate the local honey. It was fermented and they went —" He twirled his finger at his temple.

"Fou," said Lorraine.

"Yes. Mad."

"Persia." Lorraine spoke the word as if sipping mead.

Antoine refilled her wine glass. He handled the bottle with a waiter's ease, turning it so not a drop was spilled. He had broad wrists and large yet refined hands with perfect nails. She'd noticed his gestures soon after he'd moved in, the way he used his thumb to indicate the number one, and the way he gestured downward instead of upward when waving you closer. "Madame."

"Merci."

They clinked glasses, the slanting sunlight refracting through the silty wine. As usual Antoine smelled of cologne, not Old Spice but something subtler, something French, she assumed, and he was meticulously shaven. She knew he used a straight razor and had a wide leather strop. She'd seen it in the bathroom. Ray inevitably nicked himself or gave himself razor burn despite all his fancy safety razors and electric shavers. Antoine's thick, wavy white hair nearly touched his collar. It was the sort of hair she imagined guardian angels would have.

Lorraine poked at the blanket and lowered her voice so Jack wouldn't hear. "I hate this place." She looked at the rectangle of lawn, the picket fence, the plum tree, the hydrangeas, the garden she'd started and abandoned. She thought of the garden at the asylum where her mother lived. She thought of Ray off at the ten-year reunion, a crowd of crowing men with crew-cuts and thick glasses.

"But the view," said Antoine.

"Ha ha." Lorraine watched him gaze beyond the yard to the North Shore mountains whose western slopes were turning rusty in the late summer sun. "That's all this place is: a view. What I don't understand is what you're doing here. Canada. Even the name sounds empty. Like an echo in a barrel. Canada. *Nada.*"

Antoine stood and walked away. The suddenness made Lorraine fear she'd insulted him. But he was smiling. "How's the view up there, Jack?" Lorraine had forgotten all about him.

"Ivor's mom is in the kitchen window."

"What's she doing?"

"Waving."

"Wave back." Then Antoine asked Lorraine, "Where should I be?"

Lorraine didn't hesitate. "Paris."

"Ah," he said, reminded that he had a little something for her. He opened the newspaper and read aloud, " 'Pious, poetic baroness found bound and nailed to her bedroom floor with an ornate Japanese dagger.' "

"In Paris?"

"In Paris."

"Is that supposed to scare me off or intrigue me?"

"I don't know." He handed her the article.

Lorraine read it. There wasn't much, just the bare facts. Her imagination filled in the rest. She envisioned the baroness bleeding on the Persian carpet while the antique clocks ticked and her Siamese cats peered from beneath the canopied bed and the woman's lover, maddened by jealousy, stood over her, sobbing, bloody hands at his sides, asking P*ourquoi? Pourquoi?* Lorraine considered that a good way to die. *Un bon mort.* She wished she'd been born in Paris in *La Belle Epoque.* If only she could claim a thwarted passion to paint or sing or dance. The problem was she didn't know what she wanted; she only knew what she didn't want, and even there she was often unsure. It seemed to her she'd missed a stage in life, that somewhere between high school and motherhood there should have been something else, a trip with a rucksack, a journey to Tangier, a season picking grapes, a summer serving drinks in a Left Bank café, an autumn in a garret gazing at the Paris rooftops, something, anything. Recently she read an article on Queen Elizabeth. Apparently she had hundreds of servants, including one man whose full-time job was to wind the clocks in Buckingham Palace. There were twelve furniture polishers, and two men who did nothing but shampoo the carpets. Lorraine imagined living in a palace with gilt mirrors and Turkish carpets and painted ceilings and a man who wound the clocks all day. She wished she could wind the clocks in Buckingham Palace.

Antoine sat back down and picked up his wine. "I think your security blanket has turned into a straitjacket."

Lorraine felt like crying. She'd been seventeen when she met Ray. He was living in a one-room suite, everything organized with a bachelor's obsessiveness: his books categorized on the shelves, his shoes side by side on a mat, the LPs arranged alphabetically in wire racks, his coins piled in columns of pennies, nickels, dimes, quarters, half dollars. Framed photos of famous bridges hung on the walls: Golden Gate Bridge (San Francisco) 1937, Volta Bridge (Ghana) 1956, Lake Pontchartrain Causeway (New Orleans) 1956, Rialto Bridge (Venice) sixteenth century. Those pictures were in Jack's room now. Ray arranged his freshly washed dishes on a tea towel with an architectural eye, the cutlery laid along one side with the spoons turned down so the water didn't pool, then came the dinner plates, the side plates, then saucers sorted in descending order. Having grown up with the chaos of her mother, Lorraine had never seen such attention to detail. It was reassuring.

Only the lovemaking had been disorderly. The first time they did it his confidence abandoned him, as if they'd wandered into the woods, lost their way and he'd panicked. He knelt on her thigh, put an elbow into her ribs, snagged his watchband in her hair. When he reached down under her skirt it felt like a spastic blind man groping for coins. They were on his couch and he whacked his anklebone against the edge of the coffee table while she lost a button on her blouse and heard it bounce like a bead on the hardwood floor. He apologized and got down on his hands and knees to find it. She sat up and watched him crawl about.

She'd never noticed he had so much hair on his back.

"Ray. It's okay."

"I got it."

"Do you have any candles?"

He found a packet of birthday candles the size of matchsticks left by the previous tenant.

"Nothing bigger?"

"Should keep some in case of a power failure," he admitted.

Somehow they made it to the bedroom. He had a grand old brass four-poster, but as there was no rug their bumping and prodding sent it skating about the room. His size and heat and bristly chest were both frightening and exciting. All she could hear was their panting, as if they were running shoulder to shoulder. Then it was over, a rough but exhilarating ride rolling to a sudden stop. When he fell asleep afterward, she found him as endearing as he was disappointing.

In those days they shared an inclination to confession.

"In Aldershot I started talking like a Brit. You know, 'bit of a rum business,' 'feeling a bit knackered.' Even grew a moustache."

She cocked her head back and narrowed her eyes trying to imagine it. "What kind?"

"David Niven."

She liked that. David Niven was just the right combination of handsome and comic and rakish. David Niven was fun. "I used to practise having a French accent," she said.

"Non!"

"Oui."

Six months later Lorraine proposed to Ray. It was the morning after the first night they ever slept together without making love. A sunny winter morning in a bedroom brilliant with sunshine, the snow on the ground silencing the world except for a lone robin in a nearby tree. Not having sex had been a relief, a glimpse of what married life would hold. It was a huge step to simply hit the hay together. She woke to the scent of snow and the sound of the robin and in the distance a church bell. Ray made coffee and they lay in bed reading the paper, exchanging sections and reading out items of interest. The old couple in the apartment next door resumed an argument from the previous evening about who broke the sugar bowl. From bed Lorraine and Ray could see the icicles melting from the eaves and hear car tires spinning in the snow. Sunday morning in January. She hadn't planned to ask him. Women didn't do that. But the winter sunlight filled her like laughing gas and out it came.

❖

"We'll want to talk to your husband," said the cop.

"Of course."

"Did anyone else around here know him? Neighbours?"

Lorraine tried to think and the only ones she could come up with were Olivia and Rat, but she was sure Antoine had never said more than hello, and anyway she didn't want them involved, she didn't want them near Antoine dead or alive. Everything Olivia got her hands on became soiled. Olivia had undoubtedly spotted the police and was watching the house right now frantic for news and aching to come on over. "No.

Not really. I mean, he never mentioned any of them."

There was a knock at the front door. Lorraine's head swung around. The front door was the formal door; whenever anyone arrived at the front it meant business. From where she sat in the kitchen, she could see the front door there at the end of the hall. Her heart beat a warning in her throat.

"Excuse me." She crossed the living room with its French posters and its globe, paused, wiped her hands on her hips, then opened the door. Fuller Brush? Jehovah's Witnesses? A young man in a black suit stood there.

"Redmond Evers. Highland Funeral Services." Evers stood in a pose of professional decorum, hands folded low over his groin and head bowed. Lorraine couldn't believe it. A funeral director? Him? He was her own age, tanned and athletic and handsome. He seemed more like a water skiing or tennis instructor than an undertaker. She invited him in, wondering how he got up each day and faced corpses. Evers nodded familiarly to the older cop and even through her grief Lorraine saw that this was routine. That made her feel betrayed. Who knows, later they'd probably stop in for lunch at the Renfrew Café or the VicWay and talk football or women. They probably swapped anecdotes of the sort Lorraine didn't even want to imagine. On the way out of the restaurant they'd take mints and toothpicks from the plates by the cashier, then wade belching into the afternoon while Antoine lay in a meat locker.

"Well." Redmond Evers' tone was both brisk and solemn. He assumed the role of Master of Ceremonies and extended his arm in an usher's gesture, inviting them all to proceed with their unenviable chore. They walked single file onto the porch and down the front steps. When Lorraine spotted the hearse she groaned and vomited on the grass.

"Lorraine!"

She straightened up. The hearse had brought the neighbours onto their porches. They stared shamelessly: Gene Rosencko and his mother; Dolly Gooch; Eva and Nadia and, of course, Olivia. Olivia spied on all the neighbours and had most likely watched her and Antoine drinking wine on the lawn Saturday and invented all sorts of scandal. It was one thing when the scuttle-butt was about others, but when Olivia turned her carnivorous eye on Lorraine, Lorraine felt violated. Now, as Lorraine jack-knifed in another convulsion, she felt Olivia's cool arm coil around her shoulders to support her.

"Antoine?"

Lorraine nodded between heaves.

"How?"

"Suicide." Lorraine retched again.

"God ..." Olivia couldn't mask the thrill in her voice. "Oh, look."

Lorraine wiped her mouth with the back of her arm. "What?"

Olivia pointed to Antoine's suite. There was a snap and flash, snap and flash, as if from small explosions.

"Photographer," said the cop stepping past them and looking in the door. "Ernie. You about done?"

A new cop emerged with a large flash camera. Then they all stepped aside as Redmond Evers wheeled the gurney up the walkway. One of the wheels began wobbling wildly. Evers halted and leaned to inspect it. Then he continued through the door, nodding solemnly to Olivia and Lorraine. Even as Olivia nodded back, Lorraine suspected she was already planning her funeral wardrobe. What would it be? Black lace mantilla and full veil, long sleeves, black gloves, red coral necklace and earrings? Right now, a Tuesday morning, Olivia was wearing high-heeled slippers with red Cellophane bows, red pedal-pushers and a sleeveless red top, and had her beehive wrapped in a protective shell of toilet paper.

Olivia suddenly pinched Lorraine's forearm and whispered, "It's that Skog boy."

Lorraine spotted Egbert Skog on the sidewalk by the hearse. He was looking in the back window, glancing up at the activity here on the lawn, then peering again into the hearse. "So?"

"Shouldn't he be in school?"

"I suppose."

What with Egbert nearly burning down her garage, Olivia was more appalled than ever by the Skogs, insisting they were inbred and certain there was scandal behind their departure from Edmonton. As for the father, Olivia said Sven Skog watched her and that Rat was going to have it out with him mano-a-mano.

The snapping sound of Redmond Evers pulling on surgical gloves diverted them from the subject of Egbert Skog. Evers was visible through the doorway, examining Antoine's blackened fingertips, sniffing at him, leaning to look into his gaping mouth. Evers then reached a forefinger inside Antoine's mouth — an act of violation that made Lorraine gag as if Evers was reaching into her mouth with a rubber-gloved finger. He came out with something.

The older cop stepped in and joined him. "Whataya got?"

Evers showed him his finger. "Glass."

Lorraine called, "He had glass in his mouth?"

Evers and the cop turned and looked disapprovingly at Lorraine standing out on the lawn with Olivia.

"Seems that way," said the cop.

The two men manipulated Antoine's body onto the gurney and then Evers wheeled it outside and paused by Lorraine. "I wouldn't want to commit myself before running some tests, but I smelled bitter almonds and —" he shook his head and raised his eyebrows "— that suggests cyanide."

"And the crushed glass?"

"Well, it sometimes comes in ampoules."

"Where the heck did he get his hands on that stuff?" wondered the older cop.

Olivia led Lorraine into the kitchen, put water on to boil and set out cups and saucers for tea. Eva Skog and Nadia joined them. Eva was pregnant, wearing a faded blue maternity frock, her hair tied back with a frayed shoelace. She also had a black eye and cut lip. Lorraine didn't know whether to express concern or pretend not to notice. She saw Olivia was having the same dilemma. Lorraine knew Sven beat Eva; no sooner was one set of bruises fading than he gave her another. Lorraine had never spoken to Sven Skog; she saw him though, his posture sullen and his shoulders sloped, eyes small and mean as blood blisters.

Olivia busied herself pouring the tea and Lorraine watched as Nadia dug her spoon into the sugar bowl one, two, three, four, five times.

Eva, in a tone so flat she might have been discussing cleaning products, said, "My father committed suicide." Gazing past them at the still life with pheasant on the wall, Eva described the shotgun and the blood and the smell and the mess. "We were finding bits of bone and hair for weeks." As she talked, she draped a hank of her hair behind her ear. Her lip was not only split but chapped. Lorraine noticed a thin scar running across the inside of Eva's wrist.

"Why did he do it?"

"It was just the way he was."

Just the way he was.

"But Antoine always seemed so ..." Olivia struggled for words. "Tip-top." She looked to Lorraine.

Lorraine looked away. She wished Olivia would go home. Olivia managed to trivialize everything. Even during a crisis and on her best behaviour with the best intentions she reduced the world to farce. Lorraine decided that if Lucille Ball ever tried a serious role then she would be like Olivia, a pathetic parody, touching only in that she fell so short of the mark.

Lorraine saw Eva and Olivia not so much as friends offering solace but as two possible futures: Eva ruined at thirty-three by childbirth and a drunk husband, and Olivia having wasted her life in the very place she swore to leave. Lorraine knew Olivia spent her days battling the hair overrunning her chin and upper lip — she'd caught her at it one morning when she'd popped over to return a roasting pan — and the rest of her time watching TV — *that Desi Arnaz is so sexy*. She alternately lamented and clung to her affair with Rat Gardecki, even though she considered herself above him and was embarrassed by the fact that his hands were permanently grease-blackened. On good days she reassured Lorraine — and therefore herself — that soon "Rollie" would get a job out at the airport and they'd have free airline tickets, which meant weekends in 'Frisco and jaunts to Acapulco and Montreal and New York. On bad days she resolved to chuck it all and move to L.A. and take her chances as an actress. After all, she said, she didn't want to end up like Dolly Gooch, living for bingo at the Eagles Club. The neighbourhood was full of people like Dolly and Eva and clubfooted Gene Rosencko next door, people going nowhere. Lorraine knew Olivia fancied herself "a stunner," with a Hollywood bone structure. She'd plucked her eyebrows and redrawn them in a high sexy arc emulating Claudette Colbert in *The Palm Beach Story*. And she made no secret of admiring Ray's Thunderbird.

Ray. Again she wondered what he was up to, calling in sick. If he'd pulled over and called from a booth he'd be home by now. But she knew where he was, she knew. It was obvious, wasn't it? She just had to get rid of Olivia and Eva before she could do something about it.

Staring into her teacup, Eva confessed, "I tried."

"Tried what?" asked Olivia.

"With a knife. Here." Eva placed her finger on her sternum. "But the blade broke."

"Eva ..." Lorraine would never have believed her capable of such passion. She glanced at Nadia's reaction to her mother's admission, but Nadia was occupied with scooping the sugary sludge from the bottom of her teacup and sucking it from her fingers. Nadia was like a five-foot-six-inch three year old with a voluptuous figure.

Olivia pinched the collar of her blouse, taken aback.

"The scar's star-shaped," said Eva, wistful.

As a teenager, Lorraine had contemplated suicide. It would have given her the last word and cursed her mother with eternal guilt. "Why?"

Eva pushed out her lower lip, pondered in her lugubrious way and shrugged. "Miscarriage." She shrugged again. "And another time, here." She showed them her wrist in a gesture that made Lorraine think of a clerk inviting her to sniff perfume. She began to think she'd dismissed her unfairly.

Olivia put her red-nailed fingers to her throat and said, as if trying to divert them onto a cheerier subject, "I suppose there'll be an autopsy."

The blood fled from Lorraine's face. "Why?" Lorraine heard the plea in her own voice.

"Well, to determine the manner of death." Olivia's tone implied it was obvious.

Visions of the morgue — scalpels, suction, viscera — brought on another bout of nausea.

"Have you called Ray?" asked Olivia.

"What?"

"Ray."

"He's, yes, he's on his way."

"If I found a body I'd run right down to Rollie's so fast." Olivia shuddered and lit another Belvedere. "He's good that way. He can handle emergencies. All that time in the air force." She looked at the clock on the stove: 11:05. "When did you call?"

"Just a while ago ..." Lorraine gestured vaguely, thinking about Antoine being dissected.

"Maybe I should call Rollie," suggested Olivia.

"What?"

"Rollie."

"No. Ray'll be here."

"You're sure?"

Lorraine hated her now. "Yes, Olivia. Yes!"

"I'm sorry. It's just —"

"Just what, Olivia? Just what?" Lorraine was half out of her chair wishing it was Olivia who'd poisoned herself. Then she felt like a fool because it was obvious Olivia knew something; she was dropping hints on purpose. Lorraine sat back down and faced it: Charlene was on holidays and Ray had called in sick. Ray and Charlene, Charlene and Ray. Ray — solid, reliable, secure Ray. She knew it, she could feel it: the bastard was having an affair, screwing around, doing it. And here was Olivia watching — studying — the impact of the fact on Lorraine. It was obscene. "Are you that bored, Olivia? Is your life so dried up and useless, you old —" She sobbed.

Olivia patted her hand. "There, there." Fat, smug sympathy oozed from her voice.

"I watched him from the kitchen window," said Eva. "Antoine loved you. It was obvious."

There were two pops. They all looked and saw two of Lorraine's fingernails had snapped from gripping the table edge.

The man she loved had killed himself; her husband who wanted her pregnant was having an affair. She was losing everything. She didn't want the life Ray wanted, but it was hers, Ray was hers. She'd paid for him. She found herself suddenly valuing him more highly now that someone else was after him. Charlene. Lorraine had met her. She had boobs like Jane Russell's.

"That's interesting," said Olivia in an airy tone of voice. "I noticed Antoine looking at me." She sniffed. "Rollie noticed, too."

Lorraine's urge to bash Olivia across the skull with her teacup was cut off by Eva flinching and placing her palm on her swollen belly.

Olivia asked, "Are you okay?"

Eva nodded quickly.

Lorraine thought of Egbert and Ivor and Nadia — Nadia was blowing bubbles now with her saliva. She feared ending up like Eva Skog, servant to a scabrous spawn of Ivors and Egberts and Nadias. Lorraine had seen Eva at the public pool. Eva didn't wear a bathing suit but an old brassiere and a pair of blue gym shorts, making no attempt to hide the red stretch marks left from eight pregnancies in ten years. She'd had two stillbirths and three miscarriages and three children. Lorraine's own figure had returned after having Jack, but how many more kids before she ended up looking like a sack? She'd been in Eva Skog's house — more cattle pen than home — and seen the gouged walls, the charred floor, the peeled wallpaper, the torn drapes. At first Lorraine had believed Egbert and Nadia were a cruel cosmic prank played upon a woman too bovine to comprehend the notion of contraception, that maybe Eva was so backwoods she didn't understand the connection between sex and pregnancy. With the revelation of her suicide attempts, Lorraine now thought differently. And now here was poor Eva Skog watching her belly swell for the ninth time.

"I suppose I should have had babies," observed Olivia, gazing at the bloody-mouthed pheasant in the picture.

"I'm sorry. I have to lie down." Lorraine stood, reeled from light-headedness — stars popping before her eyes, sweat chilling her skin — and reached for the table to steady herself.

"Do you want a Valium?"

"No."

"To relax?"

"I just need to lie down."

"I'll stick around," said Olivia.

"No, no, go home. Please. Ray'll be here soon." Lorraine tottered from the kitchen into the living room and on toward the bedroom. She closed the door then leaned her back against it. *Did I know all along?* she asked herself. *When did I first become suspicious?* She made it to the bed. Ray and Charlene. Her mother had once said Lorraine's dad played around.

"Yes, your dad was a bit of a lad," she'd remarked, reflective and malicious at the same time.

Lorraine had refused to believe it. There had always been a nobility to growing up with a dead father. My dad died in the war, she'd say. That was a sacrifice, and Lorraine felt like a martyr. Her visions of his brave death on the smoking battlefield beneath the storm clouds bore Napoleonic grandeur. Ray had understood that.

Ray, it seemed, was a bit of a lad too.

And it was her fault. After all, if she were doing it right, if she were satisfying him, if she were a real woman, then he wouldn't be going elsewhere, would he? The thing was, she didn't know what she was allowed to expect of marriage, of Ray, or anything else for that matter. More importantly, Lorraine didn't know what she was *allowed* to feel. Did it mean she was frigid if she wasn't in the mood? Was she supposed to get herself into the mood and always be ready? Wasn't it Ray's job to get *her* in the mood? Wasn't that romance?

Lorraine had only discovered orgasm the year before, by accident, in the bathtub. She'd idly propped her feet up the wall and lay back as the tub filled, but the running water touched her between her legs in a place that had never known much attention. She'd sat up, glanced guiltily around, then done it again. It was as if she'd bumped a secret switch from a Sherlock Holmes novel and the bookshelf opened revealing a room full of delights. She began exploring that room, furtively at first, but thoroughly, very thoroughly, and often wondered if other women were doing the same.

She began paying more attention to magazines like *Chatelaine, Redbook, McCalls*. She found an interview with

Betty Friedan and was disappointed such a frumpy-looking woman had written *The Feminine Mystique.*

Ray saw the book and referred to it ever after as The Feminine Mistake.

When Lorraine heard the back door close and was sure Olivia, Eva and Nadia were gone, she stood up, opened the bedroom door, got the phone book from the shelf, found Charlene Naismith's number and dialled it, not allowing herself to pause or hesitate or even think. She held her breath while it rang. When Charlene answered, Lorraine said, "Tell Ray Antoine's dead," then hung up.

10

The Little Man at the Wheel

"Dead?" Ray lowered his glass of rye. "Antoine?"

"That's what she said."

"Lorraine? That was Lorraine?"

"What did I just say?"

"How did she know to call here?"

Charlene gave Ray a look. "You probably made a note on your calendar and underlined it in red ink."

"Jesus, Charlene."

"Well, she's your little wifey."

"Did she say anything else?"

"Just 'Tell Ray Antoine's dead,' then she hung up. Gimme my cigarettes."

Ray passed her the pack of Matinées and watched her slot one between her lips. Her lipstick was smeared like she was bleeding from the corner of her mouth, or as if he'd slapped her. He'd never slapped her, or Lorraine, or Jack, or anyone. He wiped at his own face and looked at his fingers. Lipstick.

"How?"

"I don't know, Ray."

Stroke? Car accident? ... Suicide? The last possibility made him squirm like he had worms in his belly. He saw the basement suite splattered red. No, never. A stroke. It had to be a stroke. He imagined Lorraine discovering it, her hands leaping to her face, her scream, while here he was ... "Oh, God."

"Here." Charlene plucked a tissue from the Kleenex box.

Ray wiped the lipstick from his fingers and mouth then looked at Charlene seated on the side of the bed in the pink silk negligee he'd bought her; the light from the black panther lamp slipped across the fabric's folds as she leaned toward the matching black panther lighter on her side table. On the wall was a poster of the running of the bulls in Pamplona, Spain, and that Picasso with the guy who has both eyes on the same side of his face. Other than that the walls were covered with Charlene's own charcoal and pastel landscapes. She was taking a correspondence art course with a goateed Hungarian named Jon Nagy. As well as the landscapes, she'd done full-length sketches of Ray reclining naked on the bed and had even sketched the Thunderbird.

She looked at him. "Well?"

"Well, what?"

"Well, what are you going to do, Ray?"

He stared at the lipstick-stained Kleenex in his hand.

Charlene shook her head and lifted a slat of the venetians. A bar of sunlight struck the opposite wall, then winked out when she let the slat drop. "It's beautiful out. Let's go for a drive. A long drive. It'll do you good. You can think and I can take some pictures."

"Pictures?" Five minutes ago Ray would've said great. He was always up for a cruise in the Bird. He threw back the gold chenille bedcover. "He's dead!"

"And Lorraine knows you're with me and there's nothing you can do about either of these terrible facts, Raymond."

He stared, appalled at her objectivity. "No, no way." He had to back up and pretend a little longer — a lot longer. "I don't believe it. She's lying. It's a trick."

"Fine. Don't believe it."

"He can't be dead." He looked at Charlene as if she'd know the answer. "Can he?"

Squinting past the smoke of the cigarette dangling from the corner of her mouth, Charlene picked up her new 35mm Rollei and peered through the viewfinder. "I'd've thought you'd be relieved. All you do is crab about the guy."

It was true. Thanks to Antoine, Lorraine was back on her France kick. Worse, Jacko worshipped him. A Frenchman, of all people to move in. A Frog. Maurice bloody Chevalier. The previous tenant had been a foul-mouthed Scot named Bertie McVee who drove night shift for Black Top cabs. Ray hadn't liked the guy, and Lorraine and Jack had been wary of him, but now he regretted raising the rent and causing him to move. He regretted having a basement suite altogether even though it helped the house pay for itself. The suite had been the deciding factor in buying the dump in the first place.

"What do you mean, relieved? The guy's dead and Lorraine knows about us!"

Charlene broke the news. "She's probably known for months."

Ray felt his brows harden. Why hadn't Charlene said something? Why hadn't Lorraine said something? "You think?"

"Yes, Ray, I think."

"And all this time —" Ray shrivelled. He was humiliated that she'd known. She'd *known* and kept her mouth shut. She'd slept beside him, had breakfast and supper with him, watched TV with him, made love to him and even joked with him and she'd *known*.

"I can never figure it out, Ray. Are you a brilliant dunce, or a dunce who's occasionally brilliant?" Shaking her head, she blew dust from the camera lens.

Ray leaned his head in his hands and dismantled the situation, then, with the parts spread out in his mind, he tried piecing them back together. Someone ratted. That nosy bitch Olivia, always out there watching, her and Rat Gardecki, nothing better to do than spy. He looked up and, wonderment in his voice, said, "She knew and just didn't say anything?"

"That should tell you something." Charlene stood, strolled to her vanity, arranged herself on the padded seat and, after studying herself in the mirror, sorted through her trays of cosmetics and began reworking her lipstick.

"Like what?"

"Like figure it out."

"The guy's dead and she knows about us."

She capped her lipstick and set it down hard. "Ray, if you want to go to her then go to her."

"Whataya mean?"

"Just what I said."

That made Ray feel worse. Charlene was forty-one and didn't usually get enigmatic on him. And she didn't bug him to leave his wife; that was a sign of the maturity a forty-one year old could bring to an affair. "Or," said Ray, realizing it even as he spoke, "Lorraine put it together herself. Just now. This morning." He reached for his underpants and, as if defending her, said, "She's smart, y'know. She is."

Staring at herself in the mirror, Charlene watched her expression go sour. She could almost see herself age, as if something in her was withering. She pinched her cigarette from the homemade raku ashtray and inhaled the hot smoke. When would Ray realize Lorraine was wrong for him? Charlene knew Lorraine didn't appreciate Ray, much less his work, because they'd talked at the Christmas party. Charlene had conducted a carefully planned interview all through the evening and it became clear, not just to her, but to everyone else at the party, that Lorraine and Ray were an odd match. Already straining at the leash, someone said. That's what happens when you rob the cradle, said another. Charlene saw Ray on the job five days a week, knew what he did, saw how creative he was and furthermore saw that he was respected. She wouldn't have him in her bed if he wasn't. Charlene also knew she could waltz on downtown to the Ritz or the Cave or Oil Can Harry's and have her pick any night of the week. That didn't seem to count for much with Ray, though, not anymore. Why couldn't Ray see how much she loved him? Or didn't he care? Was it possible? The thought ate her like an ulcer. She sucked hard on her cigarette — smoke roasting her throat — then swung around to face him.

"I guess you forgot, eh?"

Ray was pulling on his penny loafers. "Huh?"

"You jerk."

One shoe on, one off, Ray opened his arms wide in a big shrug. "What?"

"This is our anniversary."

"The guy's dead!"

"I got you a present!" Charlene pulled open one of the vanity drawers and threw a box at him. It hit him in the chest and dropped to the floor.

Ray stood looking at it. The wrapping paper was white with little red Thunderbirds. "Our anniversary?"

"A year ago today."

Ray was astounded. A year? Already? "No way."

"Yes."

He made a face like he didn't believe it.

She slammed the vanity drawer shut. "God, I hate you."

He tried to go to her, still wearing only one shoe, but she moved, putting the bed between them. "Charlene ..."

She mimicked him. "Ray ..."

He sat down and pulled on his other shoe, then tucked his shirt in, recalling the Monday morning last September when

Charlene first appeared behind the receptionist's desk in a tight red sweater and black tweed skirt looking like Ava Gardner. On Friday of that first week they went for lunch at the Pompeii, then cruised Stanley Park in the Thunderbird, found a secluded spot and did it in the back seat beneath the fir trees. Charlene loved the Bird. She loved the tuck and roll all-leather interior, the dashboard, the zinc knobs. "It's got great lines," she'd said, appraising the car with her artistic eye. When Ray spoke of going for the big glide down to Vegas, Charlene nodded yeah, getting all worked up. That's what did it for Ray — the fact that Charlene could see, really *see* the Bird and feel that hot desert wind.

In bed Charlene was more enthusiastic than Lorraine. She was hot. She marvelled at what great skin he had. She got off on simply touching him. That made him more relaxed and adventurous. Add to that the illicitness, the secrecy and he got so hard it felt like he had three legs. With Lorraine it was awkward. It felt more like a doctor-patient relationship and Ray knew they were both relieved when it was over, as if sex was some sort of surgical procedure. That angered him. It hurt him too, and he didn't know how to deal with it except to conclude Lorraine was young and didn't know what she wanted. Charlene did know what she wanted — *him.* "I'm sorry."

"Yeah. Me too." After a silence, she said, "You better go home. She's ... she's going to need some help."

He nodded.

While Charlene wanted Ray, she didn't want an enemy in Lorraine. She thought of Lorraine phoning her home. Could she expect a nasty little visit, too? Lorraine seemed sweet enough, but that was deceptive. Charlene had had enough enemies and nasty visits, and she knew that Lorraine would blame her. It was natural. She felt lousy for her and was almost tempted to give her a call herself. "She's too young, Ray."

"She's my wife."

"She's a kid."

"She's twenty-four and the mother of my son."

That shut Charlene up. She was hurt yet impressed. Why couldn't he be that adamant about *her*?

"And she will be the mother of another son or daughter," Ray added, with prophetic solemnity to cover the fear that Charlene was right. Why couldn't he and Charlene have met ten years ago? He'd have married her, but it was too late for that. He wouldn't break up the family because of what it would do to Jack. Anyway, he liked things as they were. Sure, he wished it were better, but even if he and Lorraine were perfect he'd still want Charlene. And why not? Ray viewed it as healthy, even Zsa Zsa said so. Hell, rumour was Jack Kennedy had poked Marilyn Monroe and everyone knew Sinatra had them coming and going and what about Hughie Hefner? Yeah, Ray hated the guy's face, but he'd be the first to admit he was progressive. The bugger was all women this, women that.

Ray couldn't bear imagining what Lorraine must be feeling now. On the other hand, he maintained defensively, maybe if she wasn't so lippy he wouldn't be here with Charlene at all. The fact was, they'd been on a different page for a long time, and this was going to take some serious retooling to straighten out. She'd caught him, nailed him to the wall, and it required prompt action.

He looked around, taking in the bed, the white shag carpet, his penny loafers, the Moulin Rouge poster, Charlene at her vanity watching him in the mirror, and he realized the simple and obvious solution — they should take that trip to France. Do it. Go. Get it out of Lorraine's system. Maybe things could turn around for them. She'd wanted to go since the day they met. "We're a family," he said as much for himself as for Charlene.

Fresh cigarette clenched between her lips, Charlene raised her hands and offered three claps of applause. "Hip hip hooray. The honourable husband declaring his allegiance. What a straight-up guy, Ray."

Ray felt like a goof. "What do you expect?"

"From you — nothing." Inside, however, she was crushed. All her life she'd been the other woman. Now she was middle-aged and desperate to get something going. She sincerely believed Ray and Lorraine were heading for Divorceville and that she was the more suitable mate for him. She wasn't giving up. Not now. Not this time. "So. Ray," she began innocently, "did you like the Beatles concert?"

Halfway into his blazer, Ray froze and looked at her, haunted. Lorraine had dragged him to see the Beatles last year at Empire Stadium. He'd sneered at the Beatles with their homo haircuts, been embarrassed when Lorraine went wacko and shrieked along with all the kids and been terrified by the crazed crowd. He'd told Charlene he figured he was the only one in the entire stadium who was relieved when the little Limey shits buggered off after only fifteen minutes on stage. "Whataya mean?"

"Me? Nothing. Just I hear the Rolling Stones're comin' to

town," said Charlene, hating herself for stooping so low. At that moment she hated Ray as much as she loved him. "So get ready."

"She doesn't like the Rolling Stones."

"No?" Charlene made a face like that was news. "That's not what she said to me at the Christmas party."

"You talked to her?"

Charlene smiled a wide sour smile thinking of Ray at the Stones. In fact, Charlene liked both the Beatles and the Stones. She liked the music and she wanted to bite Paul McCartney all over. "And they say the Stones do long concerts, Ray. None of that fifteen-minute stuff. I saw on TV where they do three hours, then two, sometimes three, encores. They did five encores in New York."

Charlene saw Ray's eyes widen with horror.

"Different generations, Ray. Different worlds. Think about it, she was six years old when you were in the army. Jack's age."

Ray considered that. His throat convulsed as he swallowed. He'd never thought of it in that way before.

At last, judging the moment to be right, Charlene tossed him a life preserver, "Me, I'd rather go see Ian and Sylvia."

Ray's face had fallen into such wretchedness Charlene worried she'd gone too far.

"Ray?"

Ray stood beside the bed in his penny loafers and blazer as stunned as a clubbed fish.

"You want a Maalox? I got peppermint flavoured."

Ray felt his mouth move on its own, far away and remote. "No."

"You sure? You look sick."

Ray shook his head.

Charlene began feeling sick, too. She continued watching him and endured the realization that whatever she'd been telling herself this past year, Ray had never — ever — said a word about leaving Lorraine. Charlene was his piece on the side and that was it. The terrible fact was, however, that Charlene had secretly been hoping to ease Ray away from Lorraine, to do it so subtly that Ray would announce the decision wholly on his own. *Best to do it now,* he'd say, *as soon as possible, while Lorraine and Jack are young enough to start over ...* Charlene felt her chin tremble and eyes fill. Was it over? Should she take a stand? Give him an ultimatum? She felt exhausted. Her shoulders sagged and she wanted another rye. She knew ultimatums. She'd gotten them and she'd given them and they never worked. She wanted to tell Ray she loved him, that they were right for each other, that it was all there, but she was afraid of scaring him off. "Aren't you going to open your present?"

Ray picked up the gift and slowly tore at the wrapping paper. It was a Dinky Toy Thunderbird. It even had a little man at the wheel.

II

X Marks the Spot

Exiled to the stool in the corner Jack felt naked and exposed. He watched the kids watch him and tried to think what to do with his face. Smile? Frown? Shut his eyes? Above all, he tried not to look scared. There was Fat Boy Burton, there was Miriam, there was Ivor, all of them over there where it was safe. Every chance Ivor got, he grinned. Jack felt betrayed. He thought of Mr. Skog and Nadia. Nadia had been whimpering. Why was Mr. Skog punishing her? Did Mr. Skog do that to Egbert when he caught him spitting in his underpants? And was Mr. Skog going to get Jack for watching? Dizzy with fear, Jack felt the floor plunge and rise. He wobbled and nearly fell over. The class laughed. Mr. Gough gave him a look and Jack gripped the edges of the stool. It was only when Miriam raised her hand and asked to go to the bathroom that the class's attention was diverted and Jack was forgotten.

Mr. Gough ceased the numbers drill. "The washroom?"

Miriam nodded, eyes round, mouth small.

Jack watched Mr. Gough make a face as if he'd never heard of something called the washroom.

"Why didn't you go at lunch?"

Jack watched Miriam panic. Crossing and recrossing her legs caused her dress to rustle and she squirmed in her seat as if her bum was itchy.

"Let me tell you how I spent my lunch," said Gough, as if embarking upon a tale. "After I dismissed you lot, I washed my hands and went to the staff room and drank a cup of coffee and skimmed the newspaper. By reading the newspaper I learned something. I learned that Albert Schweitzer died. Fifty-cent question! Who is Albert Schweitzer?" Mr. Gough pointed his stick at Miriam.

The class waited.

Jack waited. Albert? He didn't know anyone named Albert.

Nor, it seemed, did Miriam, whose response after a fit of trembling was a splatter of pee. She was seated at the front of the row and Jack had a perfect view of the pee spreading around Miriam's shiny red shoes, making them even shinier. Miriam was weeping now, her cheeks as wet and bright as those shoes, while the rest of the class strained to get a look.

Mr. Gough slapped his chalk onto the ledge, then marched

grimly to the door and gestured Miriam out. She fled. Mr. Gough stepped into the hall. "Fish!" A few minutes later Mr. Fish arrived with his bucket and mop and the ecstatic class watched as, pinch-faced and scowling, he swabbed up the mess.

It was a confusing moment for Jack when Miriam peed on her shoes. Had Fat Boy Burton peed on his shoes, Jack would have been happy because Fat Boy Burton had swallowed Jack's prize chestnut, the one he'd found beneath the tree in Olivia's yard. It was as big as a plum, brown and swirled and shiny, and Burton snatched it and put it in his mouth to hide it and ended up swallowing it. But Miriam was different. She and Jack had met a few weeks before at the library. He was sitting cross-legged in an aisle between the high walls of books staring at the story of *The Old Woman Who Lived In A Shoe*, when Miriam's red shoes appeared beside him. Hugging an armload of Dr. Seuss books, she stood there, pigeon-toed, knees scraped, belly thrust forward, frowning down at him and his book. He knew Miriam lived two alleys over and that they had raspberry bushes in their backyard because he and Ivor had raided them. Skirt like a half-opened umbrella, Miriam plumped herself down next to him and stated, "I think it looks more like a boot than a shoe." She looked at him with her big green eyes.

"She must have got it from a giant," said Jack.

Miriam frowned and sucked her lower lip as she considered that.

"And he's hunting her 'cause he wants it back," said Jack, getting excited.

"Maybe he's a friendly giant," said Miriam. "Like on TV."

Jack thought of *The Friendly Giant*. *Look up, look way up ...*
He thought of his dad's boots under the bench in the garage.
They smelled of leather and dirt and had bugs in them. "My
dad has spiders in his boots."

"My dad has sawdust in his ears when he comes home."

Jack saw Miriam had a small white snot in her right nostril.
It moved in and out as she breathed.

Sitting side by side they read through the book together,
Miriam leaning close to see the left-hand page. Her shoulder
and her hair — long and wavy and fragrant — touched Jack,
which both confused him and made him happy.

Though Jack felt bad for Miriam, he was also grateful
because she'd shifted everyone's attention from him. If *he'd*
peed while sitting up here in front of the class, Ivor would
tease him and Egbert would torture him and he'd have to
run away forever. Mr. Skog was already going to get him for
spying on him. Jack's chest tightened. He'd have to tell his dad,
which meant his dad and Mr. Skog would fight. He wondered
how they'd do it, wrestling or with fists? Mr. Skog punishing
Nadia reminded Jack of dogs humping. The first time Jack saw
dogs humping was on Ivor's back lawn last year when it was
still Miss Funt's lawn. His mom was there and she said they
were making puppies. Then Miss Funt ran out with a pail of
water and splashed it at the dogs who ran in a circle hooked
together like an animal with eight legs.

When Miriam returned snuffling from the washroom, her
blonde hair was clumped with tears, her ribbon wilted, her face
trembling, and she clutched her underpants in her fist. Mr.

Skog's underpants had been down around his knees and Nadia's had been around one ankle.

Mr. Gough resumed the lesson and Jack stared out the window, a lump of confusion and fear in his stomach that felt like he'd swallowed a baseball. Maybe Mr. Skog would make him drink wart remover. Maybe he'd cut him up with one of his saws. Jack's knees began to jump.

Mr. Gough laid his yardstick like a sword blade across Jack's knees and kept it there until they ceased their bouncing. "You are trying my patience, boy. Be still."

But it was like holding his breath or trying not to blink. Jack looked out the window at the world that was going on without him and he understood a terrible change had occurred. It was like the day his mom told him Miss Funt died and he gradually understood she was gone and someone else would take her house and no one would see Miss Funt in her gumboots and gardening clothes cutting slugs in two ever again. Now Mr. Skog would be after him. Mr. Skog who had saws and a beard and who'd clouted Egbert with a boot, and who you could hardly understand because of his up and down accent. The glint of sunlight on a pop bottle diverted Jack. He sat up higher, noting exactly where that bottle was. A Coke bottle. A big one. He'd get it after school and cash it in at Winston Begbie's store, which smelled of cool fruit and had a bell that tinkled when you opened the door and when you closed it.

Jack was a connoisseur of pop bottles. They came in three sizes: the small, the regular, and the big. You got five cents from Winston Begbie if you brought him a big. Yet Jack had discovered that the pop tasted best from the little ones. Ivor agreed. When you got a little Coke you drank it slower and tasted it more. Rat Gardecki said 7-Up and Sprite were "same piss, different bottles." Rat had a sharp face and two long front teeth and a metal crucifix on a chain around his neck. He had an eagle tattooed on his forearm that he could make flap its wings by wiggling his fingers. And he had a wooden crate of Coca-Cola bottles — the small size — next to the red cooler. Jack liked that red cooler. He liked the smell of it when he pushed up the lid and stood on his toes to look down inside at all the pop: Orange Crush, Pepsi-Cola, Coca-Cola, Hires Root Beer, Sprite, Tahiti Treat, Mountain Dew, Tab and 7-Up, each one with a distinct cap and distinctly shaped bottle. There was an opener built into the side of the cooler and all the caps dropped like coins into a drawer at the bottom. Whenever Rat cleaned them out he saved the caps for Jack, who'd run his hands through them as if they were pieces of eight. Rat showed Jack how to hold a bottle cap between your thumb and middle finger, then with a snap, send it spinning like a flying saucer. Flying saucers were from outer space. Jack and his dad always watched *The Twilight Zone*. When it was Jack's bedtime, his dad would say, *Picture if you will, a boy who has to go to bed ...*

Mr. Gough said, "Everyone hold up your crayons." Hands went up, each holding a box of crayons. Even Ivor had crayons. "Good." Mr. Gough handed out paper. Everyone got two sheets. "You're going to draw me a picture. You are going to draw me a picture of something from your house, something you know. A chair, a bowl, your brother, your dog. You will colour it in.

Right. Begin." Jack watched the class hunch over their paper with their crayons. Mr. Gough proceeded up and down the aisles with his hands clasped behind his back. Eventually he halted by Ivor's desk. He picked up Ivor's paper and studied it. "Skog ... You are drawing a toilet."

"Yes, sir."

When Mr. Gough slapped the paper back down on Ivor's desk and moved on, Ivor caught Jack's eye and then gave Mr. Gough the finger.

Jack quickly dropped his gaze to the floor. He thought of the toilet in Rat Gardecki's gas station. Sometimes Ivor and Jack went in there and if Ivor had a boner he'd show him. Boners were also called stiffies. You couldn't pee with a boner. If you did it went up.

Ivor often sang to his boner: "My boner lies over the ocean, my boner lies over the sea, oh bring back my boner to me, to me!"

Usually Jack and Ivor went into Rat's bathroom to rinse out their pop bottles because Winston Begbie wouldn't take them if they were full of dirt. With his pop bottle money Jack bought candy. His first choice was always bubble gum: Dubble Bubble, Black Cat or Bazooka Joe. If money was tight he bought jaw-breakers at three-for-a-penny, Mojos at three-for-a-penny, or candy bananas and candy strawberries at two-for-a-penny. When he was rich he splurged and put out five cents — an entire nickel — for a box of Smarties. In the summer it was Popsicles: orange, root beer, grape or rainbow. To remove the wrapper, he blew it up like a balloon. There were also Creamsicles, Fudgsicles, Revellos, English toffee, Freezies, Drumsticks and ice cream sandwiches. Sometimes he bought liquorice cigars, liquorice pipes, shoelace liquorice or liquorice whips. There was Thrills, a gum that tasted like soap; Gold Nuggets, which were lumps of gum that came in a drawstring sack; Wrigley's Spearmint, Doublemint or Juicy Fruit, which tasted good but he never bought because you couldn't blow bubbles. Wrigley's was grown-up gum. You had to choose well or you'd waste your money. There were Cherry Blossoms, Rollos, Milk Duds, Wagon Wheels, Pep Chews, Sweet Tarts, Aero bars, Jersey Milks, Crispy Crunches, Sweet Maries, Oh Henrys, Hot Tamales, Hot Lips, Almond Joys, Mounds, Caramilks, Mars bars, Mallow bars, Twix bars, KitKats, Reese's Peanut Butter Cups and Pixie Stix that came in a spiral-striped straw containing grape, orange or lime-flavoured sugar. And of course there were cinnamon toothpicks, chocolate cigars and candy cigarettes in their own grown-up style packet, or a slab of Mackintosh's Toffee guaranteed to suck out your fillings.

Jack's visits to the dentist were frequent and nightmarish. There was the needle, then the picks and bars wedged like fishhooks into his mouth and the nauseating rubber sheet. Then came the dentist leaning in like a mad scientist with his invasion-from-outer-space drill and the hot smell of drill-burnt teeth. Afterwards, Jack would overhear the dentist telling his mother that Jack had good teeth and good gums; then he'd schedule another appointment for more drilling.

Condemned to the stool in the corner of the classroom, Jack might have passed the remainder of the afternoon in tense if tolerable oblivion had he not spotted a younger boy passing the window with pop bottles protruding from his pockets. The boy moved from garbage bin to garbage bin, and even as Jack watched he found the bottle Jack had seen glinting in the sun, the bottle he'd intended to get after school, the bottle he was living for.

Discovering Jack staring out the window, Mr. Gough turned the stool 180 degrees so that Jack now faced into the corner and the world outside was gone.

12

French Voices

When Lorraine hung up the phone she knew she'd committed herself — but to what? Did Ray mean to leave her? Should she leave him? Had the time finally come? Breathless with fear, she paced from the kitchen into the living room. Ray leaving would take the decision out of her hands, but he wouldn't leave, he was too settled. She knew how Ray liked his toys, his T-bird, his bridge plans, his gadgets, his routines and his house. Lorraine returned to the kitchen table and lay her cheek on the cool Formica, then stretched out her arms on the reassuringly solid tabletop. Besides Ray and Antoine, she was also angry at her mother, the one person she should be able to call right now for advice, but what advice could she expect from a woman in an insane asylum?

At first Olivia had looked after Jack when Lorraine visited her mother. But one morning her mother called insisting she'd seen her husband — Lorraine's long-dead father — strolling the hospital's rose garden in his army uniform and smoking a cigarette. Lorraine hadn't had a call like that in years. Lorraine reasoned with her, but Estelle was adamant and began shouting. A nurse took the phone and informed Lorraine that if her mother didn't calm down it would mean restraint. Lorraine couldn't bear the thought of her mother in a straitjacket again. Olivia was out, so she took Jack downstairs to Antoine's.

The asylum smelled of disinfectant and stale cigarette smoke. The waxed linoleum gleamed beneath the wire-caged light bulbs, the walls were pale green and the moulding repainted so many times it looked melted. She signed in at the nurses' station to the left of the door and found her mother waiting in the lounge on one of the cracked leather couches. Estelle rose and stubbed out her cigarette. Lorraine could see immediately that her mother was more energetic and animated than usual, but was relieved she seemed to have calmed down. She looked clear-eyed and cogent. She was sporting the white wool coatdress with the wide collar and shell buttons and the matching clip-on earrings that Lorraine had bought for her last birthday. Her hair was waved up and over Jackie Kennedy style and she gripped her gloves and plastic purse. This was all good; attention to grooming was a healthy sign.

"He's back."

Lorraine felt her hopefulness die. "Ma."

"In the garden."

"It's been over twenty years."

"He looks good."

"He's dead."

Estelle laughed fondly. "That army chow has fattened him up."

Lorraine took her mother's elbow and they walked the garden. Estelle described what had evolved into a grand reunion with her long-lost husband. At one time Lorraine would have been frustrated to the point of rage. She used to try to force Estelle to face reality and feel guilt over her sorry performance as a mother, but her words made no dent in Estelle's mind so Lorraine had eventually given up. What did it matter what her mother thought? Her mother was delusional. She was in an asylum. So they drifted slowly along the paths, Lorraine once again her mother's caretaker, supporting her, indulging her, giving her the attention she craved, and hoping some new bit of information about her father, Private Ken Gerard, might slip through the veil of fantasy.

Startled crows gusted from a dogwood. Estelle shielded her brow with her gloved hand and gazed as if at a vision of larks. "They're his favourite bird."

"Crows?" Lorraine thought their low black skulls looked like German army helmets.

"They have such smokers' voices," said Estelle, fondly.

Lorraine thought crows were flying pigs. She listened to their crabby *caw caw*.

"He likes that. He wants a deep voice. Like Raymond Burr." Estelle tucked her chin into her throat and spoke in a deep low tone. "He wants a Raymond Burr voice."

Lorraine was used to this. Yet a question that had long intrigued her came to mind. "Mom. Did Dad know you were pregnant?"

"Geese." Estelle pointed up.

Lorraine didn't look at the geese. "Before he volunteered," she said, keeping Estelle on topic. She knew her mother had received the news that her father was Missing in Action in her eighth month of pregnancy, but didn't know whether or not he'd been aware, when he volunteered, that he was going to be a father. "Ma, did Dad know you were pregnant before he volunteered?"

"You can't eat those geese," she said disdainfully. "They're stringy. We used to eat goose at Christmas in Ontario. Grain-fed goose. You don't get good goose back here." She dismissed the flock disappearing beyond the trees, then tried to light a cigarette, but her suddenly trembling hands couldn't get the match lit so Lorraine did it for her. Estelle took the cigarette and smoked as if sucking oxygen.

Lorraine saw her mother's energy fading. She was slowing down, becoming doubtful. This was the Estelle that Lorraine had become used to visiting over the years: delusional, then depressed, then manic, then tired and lost. She took her mother's chin and turned it so they were face to face and repeated the question. "Did he?"

"Does he what?"

Lorraine was patient. "*Did* he know you were pregnant?" Lorraine felt cruel watching her mother's blue eyes blink and water. "Mom?"

"I keep telling him to get a job at the post office and be a mailman. It'll be healthy. Have you noticed how he's always pacing? I tell him, 'Take your boots off, you'll ruin the floor.' That's why I don't get down on my hands and knees and wax it. I mean, why should I?" She smoked her cigarette to the filter. Lorraine took it from her and tossed it. Estelle's hand went to her hair and her voice softened to a dreamy wistfulness. "He looked good this morning. A good-looking man. Men don't usually have such big eyes." Estelle gazed off. "He waved. Looked right at my window and waved like this." Estelle imitated a wave. "Maybe he'll become an officer."

"So he knew you were pregnant."

"Pregnant?" Estelle turned her gaze to Lorraine. "Are you pregnant? Congratulations!"

"No, Ma. You."

"Me? No. I'm not pregnant." She laughed as if she was flattered that Lorraine thought it still possible. "Though there was a Mrs. Corcoran down the street who had twins at fifty-two." Estelle shivered and looked around suddenly with a worried expression. "Are you chilly? I'm chilly. I'd like a cup of tea."

Even after all these years Lorraine couldn't distinguish between sly avoidance and sincere delusion. "We're in the sun, Ma. It's hot."

"The air's too dry in there," said Estelle. "It's ruining my hair."

"Your hair looks good. Did you do it yourself?"

"His jawline is just as good as Cary Grant's."

"So Dad knew you were pregnant?"

"She had a caesarean, Mrs. Corcoran."

"Did he know you were pregnant?"

Estelle looked lost now. She began to blink. She found her pack of Rothman's but it was empty. "I want a cigarette." She turned in a panic to Lorraine. "Did you bring me cigarettes?"

"No, Ma. I'm sorry. You called out of the blue. I rushed out here. I took a cab."

Estelle pressed the open end of the cigarette pack to her nose and inhaled the scent of tobacco.

Lorraine took the pack from her and held her hand. "Did he know?"

"No. Yes. Of course he —" She frowned and withdrew into herself. For the rest of the visit she was silent.

Instead of blaming her father for running off, Lorraine blamed her mother for driving him away. Obviously her mother must have been impossible to live with. Why else would he have run? Why else would he have joined the army when he had a child coming? The war gave him an excuse to escape the unbearable. That was why Estelle had never managed to remarry despite being a young and attractive woman. She was sick, as everyone who came near her soon found out.

From the age of ten Lorraine had filled Estelle's prescriptions, cooked the meals, done the laundry and the cleaning and explained to her mother that she was hallucinating when she saw her dead husband seated on the bus bench or cutting a lawn or sitting on the couch smoking a pipe. Coming home from school to find her mother talking to the coatrack made Lorraine sure to keep her friends away from the apartment. Even if her mother was doing well, Lorraine kept them away because she was convinced the place had a smell. It smelled "off" in the same way meat went "off." Lorraine decided her mother's brain was going off, too, like a hunk of mutton rotting in her skull, and that was the reason for her perpetual halitosis, a stink so shockingly foul it was like a smack in the nose. Her mother's finger was always black from licking it and paging through magazines until the paper became so spit-softened it dissolved. Sometimes she said the people in the pictures were talking to her. She'd argue with them. She'd get angry and roll the magazine up and beat it on the edge of the table. Or she cut out the people she didn't like and set them on fire in the ashtray so she didn't have to listen to them "talk rot."

"You're the one talking rot," Lorraine would shout. "You're mental."

That would earn her a slap across the face.

Cheek scorched, Lorraine would plead, "Ma! You're talking to a picture in a magazine!"

A glimmer of realization would cause Estelle to drop onto the couch and frown at her hands as if they weren't her own, as if someone had made a switch.

"And your breath stinks from all those pills."

Estelle's pills came in translucent brown bottles and it was as if they dissolved her bones. Finding her slumped in front of the Indian-head icon on the TV screen late at night, Lorraine would lift her wrist and let it drop and Estelle wouldn't even blink. It would hit the arm of the couch like a clump of kelp.

One morning before leaving for school Lorraine hid the pills. She stood in the doorway watching her mother sleep. Estelle's snoring sounded like gravel sliding up and down an aluminium chute. One of her feet stuck out from under the covers, her right breast drooped from her slip and her hair look like roadkill. Altogether a repugnant sight. The room stank, but Estelle wouldn't open the window for fear someone would climb in, even though they were on the third floor. Lorraine spotted the cluster of pill bottles on the side table and in two seconds darted in, had the bottles and was standing in the living room hunting for a place to stash them. Under the sink? Under the couch? She studied the living room: the landscape painting of horses running away over the grassy hills, the ceramic swans on the mantel, the bookshelf cum china cabinet holding the mug of commemorative spoons, the Reader's Digest Condensed Classics and Norman Vincent Peale's *The Power of Positive Thinking*. Lorraine stashed the pill bottles behind Norman V. Peale.

That afternoon Lorraine returned from school to find Mr. Lord from across the hall listening at their door. His suspenders drooped at either thigh and he was frowning as he struggled to interpret the outlandish noises coming from the apartment. Lorraine found her mother frantic, her wits and dignity gone, her hair like something Phyllis Diller would wear. Lorraine almost laughed. She plucked the pill bottles from behind Norman Vincent Peale and pitched them at her. Estelle, betrayed, enraged, saw she had a rival female on her hands.

13

Bells

R ay scanned the sidewalk for a phone booth as he drove. He worried that even the drive across town was too long to wait, that things could happen, things out of his control. He had to call Lorraine. But of course there were no phone booths, not when you needed one. He swore all the way up Robson Street and finally pulled over across from the Gifford Hotel. He dodged a cab and pushed through the glass doors where the desk clerk smiled and folded his hands on the counter preparing to be of assistance. On the wall behind him a row of clocks showed the time in London, Zurich, Moscow and Tokyo. He thought of his father's clocks. He also thought: who the fuck cared what time it was in Tokyo, though the word

Tokyo brought to mind Vancouver sprinter Harry Jerome who took bronze in the hundred in the Tokyo Olympics last year.

"You got a phone?"

The clerk's smile faltered. "Of course, sir." He pointed. "They should have them working in —" he checked his wristwatch "— quarter of an hour. Maybe less."

A man wearing a tool belt was working on the bank of phones across the beige-carpeted lobby. "Is there a booth nearby?"

"Just down the street."

"Down?"

"To the left."

Ray went out. The street sloped away to the right — not the left. Incompetence everywhere. He headed for the phone at the corner, searching his pocket for coins as he went, pulling everything out, even the pocket itself, leaving it dangling like a sock as he stepped into the booth and shut the folding door. Frowning at his palm full of lint and coins, he pinched up a dime and discovered the slot wedged full of gum. "What?" He squinted, then scraped at the gum with the dime. Some little shithead had worked it right into the slot.

He burst out and ran back down to the Gifford and cupped his hands around his face as he peered through the glass doors. The guy with the belt was still at it and now there were people lining up. Go? Split? He hustled up the street and found another phone, but it was occupied. A couple of blocks later he reached the main library. There were phones just inside the doors. He slotted in a dime then dialled. Someone had scraped *Wayne does Dwayne* into the side of the box. At the fifth ring and no answer, Ray reached his arm out, put his palm against the wall and leaned on it. Six rings, seven rings, eight. Maybe she was in the washroom. Or downstairs. There'd be cops. Jesus. The yard could be full of cops and an ambulance and neighbours. Nine, ten, eleven rings. He looked through the glass doors at the slow, silent world of the library, a fish tank world of people drifting about between the desks and stacks with books under their arms. He hung on until fifteen, then he waited five more, then five more after that, twenty-five rings.

His heels hit hard on the sidewalk as he hurried back up the street, cursing himself because he could probably have been home by now.

"Klein. Hey! Ray!"

Ray's head jerked and his heart spasmed at what he saw — Lon Wells and Croft Stickard.

They were both wearing white shoes and polo shirts. And they were laughing. Lon said, "What'd you do, nab some old lady's bag?"

"Wanna go golfing?" asked Croft.

"Golfing?"

"We're heading out to U.B.C.," said Lon.

Ray stared.

"Well?"

Golf? They were asking him to play golf?

"C'mon." Croft had a golf tee in his mouth like a toothpick.

"Fuck you!" Ray shoved past and reached the Gifford. The carpet was soft beneath his feet as he crossed the lobby. The repairman was gone and one phone was free. He banged the dime into the slot like a puck into the back of the net. Golf. Jerks. As he dialled he imagined the goof, the kid, the delinquent little loser poking gum into the coin slot, which in point of fact was not down but up the street. One ring, two rings. He took a deep breath and talked to Lorraine, *Come on baby*, encouraging her like a racehorse, *you can do it, answer, please answer*. Thirteen, fourteen. *Oh God, Lorraine I'm sorry, honey, honest I am ...* He let the phone ring thirty-five times before hanging up.

When he stepped from the hotel onto the sidewalk he saw a meter maid letting his windshield wiper blade slap down on a parking ticket.

"Hey!" The traffic prevented him from crossing. "Hey!" He stepped out, then jumped back. "Hey!" Seeing an opening, he zigzagged through the cars like Willie Fleming cutting through the defence. But even before reaching the other side he knew it was useless. The ticket was written and she was already half a block away. He plucked the ticket from beneath his wiper blade and got in the car. His head hurt. The rye was coming back on him and the phone was still ringing in his ears, ringing again and again and Lorraine was not answering. He groaned, hugged the steering wheel with his forearms and leaned his head on them, thinking to hell with Lon Wells and Croft Stickard.

14

Dimes in Your Eyes

Lorraine watched the phone ring. She knew Ray was frantic and pissed off and scared because he didn't know what she was up to. She just sat there and watched. It was like being at the zoo in front of a leopard cage or the snake case, safe on the other side of the bars or the glass. She'd keep back, stay silent, be enigmatic, because there was power in that. That was something she'd finally figured out thanks to her absent father. When you weren't there they wondered about you; when you didn't talk, they listened.

Having a father absent somewhere over the sea had always been fertile ground for Lorraine's fantasies. Her father was off in a distant land battling dragons in his quest for the Holy

Grail. Someday he'd return in glory and triumph and tell her she was the only thing that kept him going through all those dark and terrible years.

Yet while Lorraine grew out of those fantasies, her mother didn't. Given that his body had never been recovered, Estelle had devised theories. Sometimes she believed he was alive and living in a French village with the woman who'd found him and nursed him back to health. "He's only staying there because he has amnesia." Sometimes the woman was young and beautiful and Estelle would blink and frown and go silent. Other times it was an old woman and he was forlorn. "We have to find him. We have to contact Interpol." Or Estelle forgot the war altogether and said he was working overseas. Or he was simply doing shift work and would be home late, and in a whirl of wifely efficiency Estelle would cook a roast and then sit at the table and drink an entire bottle of wine herself as she waited, watching the candles drip and burn down and the flames die in puddles of wax.

Lorraine never let anyone come over to the apartment, but she was always eager to see how others lived: roast beef at six with families who said grace, laughter and jokes and gentle teasing, easy conversation, the ritual passing of the gravy boat, cheerful fathers and efficient mothers, brothers and sisters and babies, then after supper everyone gathered before the TV to watch the *Wayne and Shuster Hour*. This only reaffirmed her fears of her abnormality and isolated her further. Friendships were fleeting enthusiasms that died due to Lorraine's panic at being exposed, and for this too she blamed her mother. *On n'est pas comme les autres.*

Lorraine discovered the only thing worse than a drugged mother were the times Estelle decided to clean herself up and rejoin the world. She'd drag herself from her fog, smear lipstick around her mouth, resurrect her hair, then bus across town to the Arlington Cabaret to hunt a man and drag him back to her bed. Lorraine would plug her ears with her thumbs so as not to hear her mother's gin-slurred pleading and the excuses of the men desperate to escape. They'd back their way out the door with their shoes in their hands and head down the hall, leaving Estelle to stumble about the living room talking to herself, talking to her missing husband, talking to the horses in the picture running away over the hills. Lorraine filled sheets of paper with the oath: *I will never become like Estelle.* By the time Lorraine was sixteen, older girls were reporting her mother's antics at the Arlington. They called Estelle Gloria Swanson behind her back, and their boyfriends bought her drinks to egg her on. Those same guys, assuming like-mother-like-daughter, decided Lorraine was a slut — *Hey honey, hey baby* — driving her yet deeper into isolation.

Estelle's dementia peaked the afternoon she appeared wearing only a nightgown and one slipper in the hall of the high school. Banging classroom doors, she cried Lorraine's name, insisting Nazis had him in a camp. Thrilled by the diversion, the students poured into the halls despite the attempts of the teachers to keep them in check.

"Ma!"

"He told me!"

Lorraine, horrified, tried leading her away. "Who, Ma? Where?"

Estelle halted and looked around as if she suddenly couldn't recall who she was much less where. She was oblivious to the crowd of gawking kids encircling them. She smelled of urine, her hair was wild, her scalp scabbed with dandruff, and she swayed as if drunk. Lorraine, cheeks scorched by humiliation, feared her mother might vomit or pee herself.

"Ma?"

"Here." Pulling a copy of *Chatelaine* from her housecoat pocket she said, "Your father. He's in here. He told me."

"Told you what?"

"All about the crows." And right there in front of everyone — the students, the teachers, even the janitor — Estelle went, "Caw! Caw! Caw!" earning a great round of applause.

Lorraine towed her mother toward the door while the principal called an ambulance and the teachers herded the kids back into their rooms. Lorraine wanted to hide, to die, but she did her duty and accompanied her mother — strapped to a stretcher — to the Vancouver General Hospital psychiatric ward. Later, in an office, Lorraine described Estelle's delusions to a severely shaved man in a lab coat who spoke in a Slavic accent. His plaque said Dr. Kis, with a strange marking above the "s."

"And the magazine?"

Lorraine passed it to him. It was mangled.

"Which picture?"

"Page seventy-one."

Dr. Kis licked his finger and found the page. His eyebrows went up and the corners of his mouth went down, giving his face a jowly, skeptical expression. It was a drawing of a handsome Allied soldier standing forlorn at a barbed wire fence and gazing into the distance, the drawing style similar to sewing pattern illustrations. It accompanied a short story: "The Letter."

"She has done this before?"

Lorraine nodded.

Over the next few weeks Lorraine and Dr. Kis spoke several times. Each time she sat in his office she noted the wall of leather-bound books, the cast glass paperweight in the shape of a brain, the picture of his wife and five kids and the soccer trophy. He had a gold wedding band and long, hairy fingers. Lorraine couldn't keep her eyes off those fingers because the hair made her think of spider legs. Beneath his lab coat he wore a black suit and red tie and from his ear lobes sprouted more of that long, dark hair. Even more disturbing were his eyebrows that met to form a solid black hedge. But he had a soft voice, an apologetic smile and an endearing way of shyly inclining his head as he spoke that made her trust him; he was a man she could imagine as a boy.

"Your mother is psychotic. You understand the term?"

Lorraine nodded, then shook her head, then finally shrugged.

"She fails to discriminate between stimuli arising within herself and stimuli received from the external world. Therefore *your* reality, *my* reality, is not *her* reality. She is —" he looked at his hands clasped on his blotter as if they might hold the word he sought "— *divorced* from reality. For this there are multiple causes, or let us say triggers. In her case the trauma of her husband's death. She hears voices and hallucinates and talks to photographs." He frowned and considered Estelle's file. "She says she is an orphan."

Lorraine nodded; her mother had been raised in an orphanage until the age of sixteen.

Dr. Kis made a note. "She employs self-deception in order to distort her environment into a more satisfactory form. We will work toward a more rational orchestration of this relationship. It will take time, but I am hopeful." He smiled his shy smile. "I am always hopeful."

She felt obliged to smile back at him. They shook hands and he opened the door for her, almost gallant in an Old World way.

Lorraine went into the lavatory down the hall and promptly vomited. She hated the word lavatory; it made her think of laboratory — la-*bor*-a-tory — pronounced with an evil Eastern Bloc accent. She vomited because of the word psychotic. Her mother was psycho. She thought of the movie *Psycho*, Janet Leigh in the shower about to get stabbed.

Not long afterwards, Lorraine's mother was committed to Riverview Hospital. On that morning Lorraine wept with guilt because she was relieved her mother was gone.

If her mother had a reputation beforehand, her breakdown right there in the school raised her to legendary status. It changed Lorraine, too, reducing her to a stray cat, open to any and all abuse. Boys two and three years behind her shouted and threw apple cores at her. Girls looked at her, whispered, looked at her some more. She felt like Zeena Mujajic from Yugoslavia, who was ridiculed for wearing a scarf all the time, for having long, black hair under her arms and because she was a Muslim. A day never passed without a prank or a comment or a filthy note slipped through the grille of Lorraine's locker door.

✄

Lorraine's first weeks alone in the apartment were so eerie she wondered if the place was haunted. Had she inherited her mother's mental weakness? She moved slowly and stayed silent. She superstitiously left things exactly as they were, even though her mother would not be coming back for a long time, if ever. Everything sounded different: the water gushing from the kitchen tap, the whump of the flame when she lit the gas stove, the floor slats straining under her feet as she walked. She walked a lot, from room to room, listening, looking, turning as if expecting to find her mother there with an accusing look on her face. Not only did everything sound different, it looked different. She stood in her own bedroom looking at the translucent muslin curtains and the crystal dangling by a string from the curtain rod. In the late afternoon when the sun swung around, the light hit the crystal, creating a rainbow right there in her room, like a reward. She had a bed and a bureau of white-painted wood that sometimes appeared cold and alien. On those nights she slept on the couch. She kept books in a milk crate: *Alice in*

Wonderland, Through the Looking Glass, From Here to Eternity.
The row of cacti on the window ledge suddenly made her think
of barbed wire.

One evening she went through her mother's closet and in
a suitcase found her father's things: high school diploma, birth
certificate, straight razor, tortoiseshell hairbrush, silver pocket
watch, jackknife, a pair of black French-toed shoes. She'd first
found them years ago on an occasion when her mother was
passed out. Now she examined each item at leisure. She sniffed
them. Was it possible to catch her father's scent? She arranged
them in a row on the coffee table. Then she rearranged them
in a circle with the watch in the middle. The watch had stopped
at 8:08. Was that significant? She wound the watch and held
it in her hand as if it were a tiny ticking heart, her father's heart.

By the end of the first month Lorraine moved more confi-
dently. She turned up the radio and sang along with Elvis
Presley and Buddy Holly, belched as loudly as she could and
strolled naked, posing before the full-length mirror in the hall,
cupping her breasts and pursing her lips. She was also skip-
ping school to avoid the taunts. The teachers were indulgent.
More than that, she suspected they were afraid of her, fearing
she too might break down.

Then one evening gravel smacked Lorraine's bedroom window. She was sprawled naked in the chesterfield chair at the
time, legs wide — one over each chair arm — eating popcorn
exactly the way she liked it with salt *and* pepper, and reading
Othello for her English class, a scene where Iago pours poison
into the Moor's ear. When the gravel hit she flinched. The

Melmac bowl fell to the floor, where it clattered and spun to a wobbling halt. Popcorn was strewn everywhere. Fear rushed over her like bats bursting from a cave. She waited. A car went by. She was beginning to think it was nothing when another splatter hit, this time the living room window. Her head swung as if jerked by a wire. She knelt up in the chair, peered through the half-shut venetians and saw three boys in the alley. The apartment was at the back of the building and the only light came from the warehouse opposite. She could see their dark shapes and hear their coarse laughter. After a few minutes a bottle shattered and she saw them move off. Two nights later it happened again. She stood against the wall and peeked out and thought she recognized them from school, four this time, lingering by the trash cans. One peed loudly, another called her name, then they all called her name and made lewd noises. They threw pennies and pebbles and she flinched each time one pecked the glass. It was as if they were pinching her, groping her. The following week there was a note wedged under the door with her name on it: *Are you lonely up there?*

The next time the boys appeared in the alley she called the police, but the boys ran when the car arrived. Two nights later they were back. She sat on the floor hugging her knees.

Until that point she'd had little to do with boys, even though she'd watched them. She hoped that beyond the herd of crude and giddy adolescents there was someone different, someone who'd been somewhere — anywhere — a man returned from the desert or the sea or a distant city, someone who, like the French poet Arthur Rimbaud, had travelled alone and returned with a splendid dignity. Lorraine had read Rimbaud's poems but was even more impressed by his alienated life: wandering through France, taking a ship to the Far East, ten years in Abyssinia, illness, back to France, then a final, desperate attempt to return to East Africa, only to die in a Marseille hospital a few hundred yards from the port.

> *On the calm black wave where the stars sleep*
> *Floats white Ophelia like a great lily ...*

If only she could have met him.

Lorraine was soon forced to find a job because her mother's welfare got cut off and the Child Welfare contribution was meagre. She'd waitressed the previous summer at one of the Aristocratics, and managed to get hired on again. She liked it. She got to know the other waitresses and the cooks, older women and men. With them she could start over, like a new person. She liked being included in their worldly banter and she copied their gestures and manner of speech. Heading straight to work after school gave her life shape. Yet she couldn't escape completely. Among the clusters of kids who lingered in the booths she was sure she recognized the culprits who haunted the alley beneath her window. They grinned and sucked insinuatingly at the ice in their glasses. After work she bussed home, then walked the last few blocks as fast as she could. The only men she'd known were teachers, schoolboys and the men who slept with her mother: authority figures, pests and drunks. Then Ray showed up at the restaurant one evening, said he'd been to France, and the boys in the booth never bothered her again.

✖

Not only was Lorraine elevated from a teenager to an adult when she met Ray, but when she gave birth to Jack she attained, in her own eyes and those of others, solidity and status. She had arrived. Even her mother emerged from the cave of her madness to acknowledge the difference. Lorraine was relieved that Estelle showed such interest in Jack when they visited her at the hospital. Lorraine knew Jack found his grandmother entertaining, and especially liked that her purse was a treasure chest of chewing gum and pennies. She spoke to Jack as if he were an adult, sharing the ongoing scandals surrounding the other "guests."

"There's Mrs. Woo, Jack. She chews her toenails. And there's Mrs. Gibbon. She traps flies on the window and puts them in her ears. And that lady over there — see her? — that's Mrs. Riordan. She sings in her sleep."

Lorraine watched Jack's face as he heard these stories. "Don't you go putting flies in your ears."

Jack was useful on these visits. While years of Thorazine had gradually subdued Estelle's hallucinations and stabilized her schizophrenia, Jack gave Lorraine and her mother something positive to focus on.

Jack had announced that the vast brick buildings with the ivied walls and manicured grounds looked like the University of British Columbia where his dad had studied. As for Lorraine, each time she saw the asylum she was impressed by how official it looked, so stolid and stable, exactly the opposite of her mother and everyone inside.

The first time Jack visited the place, Lorraine kept him close by her side. When the weighted door shut behind them she saw him wrinkle his nose against the smell. There was scream-ing — a lone voice wailing off down a hall. Jack looked to her and she put her arm around his shoulders.

"Is this a school?"

"No, this is a —" she hesitated, she didn't want to say hospital, "— a rest home."

She watched Jack gaze down the old linoleum hall that was rippled with wear and yet shiny with wax. There was a mop in a bucket and a janitor in a white shirt and pants smoking a cigarette. Everyone smoked cigarettes. The sleepy adults in pyjamas shuffling slowly along the walls smoked, the visitors smoked, even a man in a wheelchair whispering to his fingers was smoking.

"Come on." His mother took his hand, led him down that hall and turned left into a room with two beds. In one an old woman strained and twisted against strips of sheet binding her wrists and ankles to the metal bed frame. There were bars on the window. Lorraine saw Jack's surprise at seeing a framed photo of himself on a table.

"That's such a good picture of you," said Lorraine.

Estelle appeared in a robe and slippers, carrying her false teeth in her hand.

"Mom. Hi."

But Estelle was looking at Jack. As usual she did everything slowly, as if her batteries were low. She shut her eyes and seemed to go to sleep for a moment and then opened them and smiled. "Jackie!"

"Hi, Grandma."

"How's it going, Ma?"

The woman tied to the bed groaned loudly and arched her back as if being jolted with an electric current. "Daddy!"

"Mom. We'll meet you outside." Lorraine calmly but briskly hustled Jack back along the hall past the dull-eyed adults and out the door. "Look at the trees, Jack. Look at the holly bushes!"

Jack gazed obediently at the holly bushes with their prickly green leaves. It had rained earlier, but now the spring sun shone, making the leaves sparkle, and there were scatters of birdsong. There were crows cawing and geese honking and gardeners clipping hedges. Ghostly men and women drifted about the garden paths.

Jack looked at Lorraine. "Are they zombies?"

"Shh! No."

They saw an unshaven sack of a man in a bathrobe smoking a cigarette on a bench. He inhaled, then let the smoke drift from his mouth and sucked it in through his nose, then blew it out his mouth again. When he saw them approaching he stared dull-eyed and open-mouthed.

Lorraine smiled. "Good morning."

The man's only reaction was to shift his eyes — click, click, click — by degrees to follow them.

Farther on, they heard the clattering blades of a push mower.

"It's much nicer out here," breathed Lorraine, relaxing and

gazing about. "Yes, it's a rest home, Jack. Some of the people don't feel very strong. They're tired."

"Is Grandma tired?"

"Everyone's tired sometimes. You're tired sometimes."

"Grandma's breath smells like poo."

Lorraine gripped Jack by the shoulders. "Don't be rude, Jack. That's rude. I want you to be polite. Okay?"

Jack nodded.

He was right, though, and Lorraine knew it. Poo. It was the pills and the long stretches of depression when Estelle forgot to bathe, much less brush her teeth or drink water. One thing she never forgot to do was smoke. Her fingertips were a dirty orange from nicotine. Even the doctors and nurses smoked. The sheets and blankets had burn holes, the furniture and even the walls were scorched, and smoke hung like grey gauze in the hallways and rooms.

When Estelle joined them they moved slowly uphill beneath chestnuts and cedars and sat on a bench of wrought iron and wood. Estelle did everything as if underwater.

"Are you tired, Grandma?"

She smiled. "I'm retired, Jack. Retired."

"Why was that lady tied up?"

Estelle gazed dreamily at Jack. "What lady?"

"In bed."

Estelle nodded and smiled as if he'd complimented her. "Ah. Yes. She just moved in." She placed her hand on Jack's and promised, "I'll find out who she is." Then Estelle turned to Lorraine and said, "A man died yesterday."

"Oh no. Ma ..." Lorraine's glance took in Jack's reaction but he merely listened politely.

"Drowned in the bath. Drank all his bathwater and drowned from the inside." Estelle opened her purse. It was held shut by two silver horses that interlocked at the neck. She unsnapped them, then gazed into the interior a long time.

"Ma."

Estelle blinked and came back to life. She took out her pouch of Drum. She'd recently become attached to the ritual of rolling her own cigarettes. Lorraine and Jack were forced to watch her tremble tobacco into a paper, which she then tried to lick, but her tongue was so dry from all the pills that the paper stuck to it and the tobacco spilled down her chest.

"Ma. Oh. Sorry." Lorraine pulled a carton of Rothman's from her own bag. She opened a pack, tapped up a cigarette, passed it to her and lit it with a paper match.

Estelle closed her eyes as she smoked, holding the cigarette to her lips and never taking it away from her mouth even when she exhaled. The smoke flowed up and over her face which was as blank and expressionless as a bottle. She smoked the entire cigarette before opening her eyes and looking at Lorraine and asking, "Have you heard from your father?"

Lorraine felt Jack looking inquiringly at her. "No, Ma, you know I haven't."

"I have."

"Ma."

"He called last night. Long distance. He woke me up and sang."

"You were dreaming."

She looked off at the trees. "Oh," she said vaguely, "I don't dream. Do you know there are over one hundred varieties of trees here?"

They gazed out over the asylum grounds at all the trees. Jack watched one of the groundskeepers at the rear of a truck struggle to disentangle two bamboo rakes; when the rakes wouldn't separate he became frustrated and began beating them on the grass. Like swans, the patients raised their heads and turned slowly to look.

"*God Save the Queen.* He sang *God Save the Queen.* I like the queen. Do you like the queen, Jack?"

"The queen in *Alice in Wonderland* is red and crabby," he said.

"The queen is the lady in the photograph where you check the books out at the library," Lorraine reminded him. "And she's on the pennies. Do you know her name?"

"Elizabeth."

"Good." Estelle cupped Jack's face with her hands and smiled at him.

Lorraine watched in fear that Jack might say grandma's breath smelled of poo.

Gazing into his grandmother's eyes, Jack said, "You got dimes in your eyes, Grandma."

"Jack!"

But Estelle laughed in delight and began to sing in a surprisingly melodious Peggy Lee voice, "Hey there, you with the dimes in your eyes ..."

At that moment Lorraine saw what must have charmed her father, an attractive woman with a fine voice and a lively manner. The sort of woman you could be seen with in public, a woman of grace and composure. It scared her that Estelle could seem so sane and disjointed at the same time. Madness was so close, just on the other side of the glass.

Seeing Estelle's gradual improvement over the years and noting what a sobering effect Jack had on her, Lorraine wondered if she might talk to the psychiatrists about having Estelle move in with them. She'd be a permanent babysitter and it would mean more freedom for Lorraine. She didn't speak to Ray about this. She didn't tell anyone, especially not her mother. In the end she decided it would never work. Ray would object and, more importantly, Lorraine didn't dare risk introducing Estelle to Antoine. What if they hated each other? What if she drove Antoine out? Worse, what if they hit it off?

Estelle didn't even know Antoine existed until one afternoon Jack mentioned him.

"And he has how many canaries?"

"Thirty-six," said Jack.

Estelle looked to Lorraine, who nodded that it was true. Estelle made a face, then gazed at the sky as if imagining Antoine and his birds. Then she was shaking her head as if reaching a conclusion. "No. I don't like it. Birds don't belong in cages. I don't trust anyone who keeps birds locked up."

PART THREE

THE DAY CLOSES

15
Baggage

Ray rejected the idea of buying Lorraine a bouquet of roses. The situation was beyond roses. He knew he should have said no to Gaudin moving in. He pounded the steering wheel. Rooking her down like that on the rent should have told him. From day one the guy'd been filling Lorraine's head with crap. He was probably the one who'd hinted Ray was up to something, just to mess him up, just to get in good with her, because the filthy old bastard had had his eye on her.

Ray switched on the wipers to clear away the dead bugs scabbing the windshield, but he was out of fluid so succeeded only in smearing it with guts and wings and legs. He pressed the button lowering the window and reached around with the parking ticket and wiped at the mess.

In the nearly two years Antoine had lived downstairs Ray had talked to him less than a dozen times, usually by the back steps or in the alley when washing the Bird. Antoine, the sneak, always admired the car, which meant Ray had to be nice. The last time they'd talked Ray had been rubbing mink oil into the leather seats. Antoine came huffing up the alley hugging a grocery bag in each arm, set them on the metal trashcans Ray had so meticulously painted their address on, then wiped his forehead with a hankie. Ray dutifully nodded and tried to look too engrossed in the job for conversation.

"Somebody put a lot of thought into this car," announced Antoine.

Ray thought: Who was this guy advising him on Thunderbirds? "Yeah, a team of engineers," he said gruffly.

Antoine nodded and they both admired the car. After a minute or so, Ray felt obliged to ask, "You don't drive?"

"Oh yeah, way back when."

Ray waited. "What happened?"

"Excuse me?"

"What happened? Why'd you stop?"

"I came out here."

Ray didn't follow the logic, but let it go because he didn't care whether Antoine drove or walked or crawled. "So you're bussing it."

"Yes, bussing it."

Ray hadn't been on a bus in five years, but he nodded as if to say maybe that was for the best. Each time they spoke Antoine's accent struck him as odd. Lorraine said Antoine was from southern France, which had a Spanish influence — *inflection, a Spanish inflection* — and that he'd travelled a lot. It was a Saturday afternoon in late March. Ray went at the driver's seat massaging the oil into the seams with a light circular motion, following the directions on the label. "You serve?"

"Serve?"

"The war. Europe." Ray thought Antoine might have been too old, though over there they'd taken anyone.

"Some little while."

Some little while?

Antoine coughed. "Briefly. POW."

Ray got interested. "Yeah? Where? How long?"

Ray heard the crackle of coarse paper as Antoine picked up his grocery bags. Ray backed out of the car in time to see Antoine hurrying off. Ray knew some POW camps had been pretty rough, none of that *Hogan's Heroes* bunk. Some guys couldn't talk about it. Ray had worked with one guy at Pac-Coast Plywood just after the war who had all kinds of stories, including how *Canada* was death camp slang for hope and health. *Canadians* were the privileged ones, Jews who met the trains and stripped the luggage from the other prisoners, then herded them onto the trucks bound for the gas chambers.

Squinting through the bug-smeared windshield on the way home, Ray worked on his plan of attack. Come clean? Deny? All he'd wanted was a day off. A little nooky. A poke. Then it occurred to him he could blame Lorraine. Tell her, *See, this is what happens when wives ...* But that was BS. Maybe he could blame Charlene? He sat forward over the wheel, liking the idea. He could tell Lorraine that Charlene was sick, no, stick close to the truth; that was the key to effective lying. He could say that Charlene was on vacation and Ray had to get some papers from her, something like that. Not bad, not bad. Build on that ... What about the booze on his breath? He pulled into a gas station on Kingsway.

"Just the windshield," he told the kid who ambled over.

"Mint car."

"Yeah, yeah." He dashed in and bought a pack of Dentyne. Back out on the road, he chewed three pieces into a wad, the muscles working in his temples and jaw. Or he could say Charlene called the office asking for — no, shit, it wouldn't hold water because *he'd* called in sick and Lorraine had figured that out! She'd called the office to tell him about Antoine and that Girl Friday had blown it for him. He thumped the steering wheel. He could imagine Wells and Stickard giving him the big hee-haw for getting nabbed. Couldn't even play around without getting caught. Ray wrung the steering wheel until his palms burned.

⁂

"What is this book?" demanded Mr. Gough. He paced the front of the classroom slapping the book into his palm.

Jack stopped worrying about what Mr. Skog would do to him long enough to listen to Mr. Gough. With his nose in the corner unable to see anyone or anything, it was like being blind.

"The Bible. This book is the Bible. Some day, if you are wise, you will not simply read the Bible but study it. And I will tell you why, because books are like treasure chests, and what do treasure chests contain? Burton?"

Jack heard Fat Boy Burton's voice somewhere far behind him squeak, "Treasure."

"Of course. You all like treasure, don't you? I'll wager that the Skulker Skog likes treasure. I'll bet that young Jack here likes treasure."

Jack held his breath. The class giggled. Mr. Gough chuckled.

"Seek and ye shall find," said Mr. Gough. "And if you are intelligent, when you learn to read, you will seek in the Bible."

Jack thought of his Bible. It had a secret hiding place where he'd cut the pages out of the middle, just like he'd seen in Sherlock Holmes on British Sunday Theatre. Jack had taken a steak knife from the kitchen drawer and carefully scored out the sour-smelling pages until he had a square the size of a deck of cards. He liked the idea of a book with a secret compartment. His hollowed-out Bible contained a pigeon's foot plus a French franc given to him by his dad and three gold coins given to him by Antoine. Jack had stolen the Bible from the Saint Francis of Assisi church on one of his wanders with Ivor.

Antoine also had a Bible. Jack had found it while helping feed the canaries. Antoine had to run out to the store for more seed and he left Jack in charge. The birds whirred around the room emitting pin-sharp peeps. Some flew into the bathroom and lined up along the rod holding the shower curtain, then, as if swinging on vines, they swooped from the rod to the sink. They flew back and forth along the hall carrying urgent messages. They circled Antoine's bedroom like fish in a bowl. They perched on the chair and on a lamp and one landed on the side table and pecked at a pile of coins. Jack had reached for it, but the bird whirred off. In a moment of delicious curiosity, Jack reached not for the coins, but for the drawer. It slid smoothly open releasing an odour of old wood and that's when he saw the Bible. It was heavy and limp and had a black leather cover with faded gold lettering. It also had a smell, a smell he didn't know, a smell that was new to him, like dirt and sweat and pepper. Jack opened it wondering if Antoine's Bible had a hiding place, but there were only thin pages with tiny lettering. Inside the front cover Jack saw a name written in long sloping letters in faded ink. He sounded it out syllable by syllable the way his mother had taught him. "An ... ton ... Gur ... nee ... ak ..."

❈

Saturday evening on the blanket beneath the plum tree, Lorraine had told Antoine that Ray wanted her pregnant again.

"I'll bet you're beautiful pregnant."

Heat rushed to her hips and Lorraine — scared, pleased, excited — felt obliged to contradict him. "I didn't feel beautiful."

"You were. You showed me the pictures."

"You'd be a good father," she said.

"I never found the right woman."

"You couldn't have tried very hard."

He shrugged. "I came close once."

"What happened?"

"Me. I happened."

His brow looked heavier than usual. He held his wine glass by the stem, turning it between his fingers.

"Maybe you were too young."

"And now I'm too old."

"Don't say that."

"It doesn't matter."

"It does."

Antoine blew air and shook his head.

She leaned toward him, insisting, "You're not too old." She wanted to touch his hand, to convince him.

"Ray's a good father."

"Well." Lorraine let that go. She noticed how careful Antoine was never to criticize Ray, whose idea of fatherhood was monitoring Jack's development: Jack using a spoon; Jack's first steps; Jack's first words. He'd even devised mazes out of cardboard boxes and timed Jack as he crawled his way through. Or was she being unfair? She suspected Ray's desire for another child had a lot to do with settling her down and keeping her occupied.

Edith Piaf ended and Lorraine heard the next record drop and crackle. *A Hard Day's Night.* She'd shown Antoine the cover and he'd looked bemused by the four mop tops and the words *Smart. Irreverent. Electrifying!* Now, with the opening guitar crash and those first words: *It's been a haaaard daaay's night!* Lorraine drew the elastic from her hair, freeing her ponytail. She tossed her hair in what she imagined was the French manner; her hair was the same colour as Simone Signoret's.

"Better?" asked Antoine.

"Much."

"You have beautiful hair."

Lorraine smiled and hoped she wasn't blushing. "So do you."

"Ha."

"Silver fox."

"Old fox," said Antoine.

"You're not old." Lorraine said adamantly.

He looked past her and said, "Hello."

Lorraine turned and saw Ivor in the yard, probing his ear with one finger, while with the other hand he plucked at his crotch.

Jack scrambled down from the plum tree and the two of them headed over to Ivor's to watch *You Asked For It* and *Gilligan's Island*, Jack's two favourite shows.

"I met the other boy," said Antoine. "The brother, the one you always talk about."

"Egbert."

"Yes."

"They might as well put him on death row right now," said Lorraine, assuming Antoine would agree. "It's only a matter of time."

But Antoine shook his head. "He's young."

"He's malignant."

"No. There's time."

Lorraine didn't like disagreeing with Antoine. Her voice became plaintive. "He's already been up on assault charges."

"Boys fight."

"He got expelled from every school in Edmonton. He tried

setting Olivia's garage on fire last week." She heard her evidence making a solid case. What could Antoine possibly say?

Nonetheless, Antoine remained unconvinced. He sipped his wine, brooded, then described how he'd come home the day before and found Egbert Skog looking in his window.

Lorraine, feeling violated, cut in, "He was *here*?"

Antoine nodded. "I came up behind him and looked in the window too. When he saw my reflection he just turned and demanded to know what kind of birds they were. I said canaries. He asked if they could talk. I said, 'Canaries don't talk, they sing.' He said, 'Crows can talk if you cut their tongues.' I asked how he knew and he said because he'd done it."

"See."

"Do you know what he said when I asked him his name?"

"Do I want to know?"

"Lee Harvey Oswald."

"God."

"I said he'd better go home, but he said he didn't want to go home, he didn't have a home, he had a box."

"A box." Lorraine shook her head. "He's demented."

"When I opened the door one of the birds flew out. It flew right to Egbert and landed on his shoulder. And do you know what?"

"Is it going to make me sick?" Even as she said this she knew by Antoine's look of impatience that she was frustrating him, that she was fighting the entire spirit of what he was saying.

"He looked afraid."

"The bird?"

"Egbert."

"Egbert?"

Antoine nodded. "Then he got curious because the bird stayed on his shoulder. He calmed down. All that anger left him. I watched him take the bird in both hands and look at it closely, right in its eyes. He said, 'What if I let it go?' 'A hawk will eat it,' I said. He thought about that."

"I'll bet he did."

"Then he gave it back to me. Like this." Antoine held out both hands cupped together as if in a ritual offering of sacred wine.

"So what, Goering liked dogs."

Antoine looked angry.

It was the first time Lorraine had ever seen him angry and it scared her.

"Goering wasn't a kid."

"Sounds like you've made a new friend." Now she was angry, too. Here they were drinking wine on the lawn on a summer evening and they were talking about Egbert Skog and Herman Goering. She wanted to talk about Antoine; she wanted to talk about France. "Do you ever think about going back to France?"

"Maybe he'll change himself."

"And maybe Ray will grow his hair and say, 'Let's move to Mexico.'"

Antoine said nothing for a moment, then he began laughing. Lorraine began laughing, too. "I'm sorry."

"No, I'm ruining everything."

"I wish Hurricane Frieda had knocked down every house

around here," she said. "Just flattened the whole city." Now she was laughing and crying at the same time. Antoine was grinning. She felt like laying her head in his lap. She wished he'd take her to bed. The urge scared her, but there it was, and why not? Antoine knew more about her than Ray ever would. When Antoine looked at her he saw *her,* while Ray saw only a wife and a mother or, as was too often the case lately, an aggravation. Lorraine wanted to give herself to Antoine. She wanted to lie there and have him unwrap her. Breathing hard now, her face hot, she waited for him to understand this, for him to do something. Heart thumping thick in her throat she looked at Antoine, her eyes urging him on and not giving a damn if Olivia or Eva or anyone else was watching. She reached out and put her hand on his. The evening light and the city noise receded, leaving just the two of them there on the grass with an empty bottle of wine and the last warmth of swiftly fading summer. She shut her eyes, parted her lips and leaned toward him.

Antoine slid his hand from beneath hers and gave it a paternal pat.

Lorraine felt like doused fire. She was embarrassed and insulted. *Am I that ridiculous? Am I so beneath your consideration?* She looked away, then she confronted him. In a voice both angry and pleading she asked, "What's wrong?"

He exhaled hard, as if cornered. "You make me forget."

"Forget what?"

"I don't deserve that."

"What are you ... what are you talking about?"

"When you want to punish yourself you make someone who loves you hate you."

"Why? Who hates you?"

He became vague and evasive. "I'm sorry. Nothing." He picked up his glass, set it down, gestured dismissively. "It's the wine. I'm just mumbling."

She reached again for his hand. "Antoine, I'll leave Ray."

For a moment he seemed to reconsider. "And what will Jack think?"

"He'll —" She didn't know what Jack would think. "He's a kid. He'll adjust."

Antoine began packing up. Lorraine watched him stack the plates and food and glasses in the wicker basket. Why was he doing this? Where was he going? When he stood so did she. It was all drifting away. She was already alone, the evening a dream lost to waking. He faced her and in the twilight his white hair no longer haloed his head, but put her in mind of a photographic negative. He hugged her. She tried pressing close, but he held her at arm's length.

"They say you can't lie to yourself. They're wrong."

"Antoine —"

"Good night." Antoine raised his hand as if he was on a boat drawing away from the dock.

⸬

She recalled that wave now and raised her own hand to see how it felt. It felt terminal, like he knew he was never coming back; he'd known even then what he planned to do.

Lorraine suddenly remembered the suitcase.

She went to the hall closet and brought it to the kitchen table. She peeled off the envelope. Inside was a black-and-white photo of a smiling Antoine, younger — thirty-five — but clearly him, in a uniform, with a rifle over his shoulder. Behind him ran stripes of barbed wire, and behind that stood a rail car, outstretched hands protruding between the broken planks in gestures of pleading. They stuck out at all angles, fingers splayed, blindly groping. She'd never seen so many hands and arms and fingers.

Lorraine stared at the picture, gaze shifting from Antoine's face to the barbed wire, to the arms, as if it were one of those visual tricks, a pattern of coloured dots hiding an image. Antoine was laughing the laugh of a confident man among trusted friends. Antoine had good teeth and a broad smile and nothing to worry about. She could tell the sun was bright by the shadow and light on his face. He had a strong nose and square forehead and dark eyes. She saw him there on that brilliant winter afternoon beneath a sheet-metal sky, the leafless trees as black and twisted as the tormented hands behind him. She lay the photograph face down on the table. On the back was written: "Treblinka – 1942." Nausea rumbled inside her like an approaching train.

She put her thumbs to the suitcase locks and pressed. The latches snapped up like jaws. The lid released a smell of ink and paper and iron. It took her a moment to comprehend what she was looking at. Money. She picked up a bundle of Canadian ten dollar bills. She picked up a bundle of French francs. There were Deutschmarks, pounds, but mostly American dollars, flaps of fives, tens, twenties. The bills were tied with coloured ribbons like billets-doux.

In one corner of the suitcase lay a royal-blue Seagram's whisky sack with gold lettering and a gold drawstring, the sort Jack kept his marbles in. Lorraine picked it up and felt its weight. She undid the drawstring and peered inside and saw gold. Gold nuggets. She poured them into her palm. No. Gold teeth and gold fillings, all shapes and sizes, molars and eye teeth, crowns and caps and plugs. For a moment she imagined the teeth of some mythic creature, a dragon, then she recoiled and thrust them back into the sack as if they'd scorched her skin. She stared at her palm and wiped it on her skirt. She dropped to the chair and tasted bile burning her throat. Teeth. *Human teeth.* Newsreel images spun through her mind — Dachau, Auschwitz, Treblinka — she reached out to steady herself and felt the Formica cool under her palm. In her nostrils the smell of the money lingered as pungent as blood. Antoine.

She thought of Jack alone with him. Antoine. She thought of all the times he'd babysat and she thought of Saturday night. Antoine. Dead on the couch. Antoine, Antoine, Antoine.

The sound of a car crawling up the alley — tires crunching the gravel — took her to the kitchen window. No, not Ray. She looked at the sack. A gift of gold and death. A reward and a rejection.

She went to the phone and listened to the insect drone of the dial tone. The sound made her feel even more alone, a solitary note that she feared would go on and on like a bad memory until she'd been lobotomized like her mother. What kind of tainted life was she supposed to live with this? What was he intending? He might as well have given her a corpse. And he had, hadn't he — *his* corpse. *Make someone you love hate you.* But why include her in his self-punishment?

She set the phone in its cradle and looked at the hand that had held the teeth. She went to the sink and scrubbed with soap and a Brillo pad. Why had she and Jack been so drawn to him? Weren't kids, like dogs, supposed to sense evil? Ray had been suspicious. He'd sensed something wrong because Antoine never got mail, had no friends, didn't work, and paid the rent every month in cash.

No, this was mad, a mistake, it had to be. Yet that was Antoine in the photo; that was Antoine. He always seemed so balanced and relaxed — even when he was enigmatic — so at ease and alluring, like on the morning they'd stood on the bridge over the railway tracks.

It was a Sunday seven or eight weeks ago. In a rare urge to exercise, Ray had taken Jack bicycling around the Stanley Park seawall and she suddenly had time to herself. Jack and Ray had waltzed out in high humour, What's-up-doc'ing each other, *I musta taken a wrong toin at Albequoiqee.* In the quiet following their departure, she heard Antoine moving about downstairs, the faucet, the cupboard, the closet door in his bedroom. It was eleven a.m. and he was getting ready to go out. She found herself listening to his movements and anticipating what he was going to do. She'd discovered by accident while scrubbing the floor that if she got down on her hands and knees and put her ear to the vent she could hear everything he did, right down to the click of a fork on a plate. She dressed quickly and waited by the kitchen window. When she heard his door open she stepped onto the back porch. She had a moment to watch him before he spotted her, and she saw he was frowning in that abstracted way he had, as if he was trying to remember a name or face.

"Well, well," she said.

"Lorraine."

She loved the way he said her name. *La-reine. The queen.*

As usual he wore a suit and an open-necked white shirt. If this was Paris, she thought, he'd be off to an outdoor café to sip a Pernod and read *Le Monde*. Maybe it was the way he had his hands in his pockets, but it struck Lorraine more than ever that he was utterly out of place in Vancouver, that he was in exile. She descended the wooden steps of the porch, one hand gliding the railing, wearing robin's egg blue Capri pants, a white blouse, her hair loose on her shoulders. In the distance a church bell rang. "Off to confession?"

He smiled.

As always when he did she sensed a solitude in his eyes, and that attracted her.

He pointed. "I'm going for a walk. Coming?"

In ten minutes they were on the path to Rain Lake. Amid the scrub cottonwood, vine maples and salal, the earth was still damp and pungent from the night. Blackbirds and chickadees whooped and piped. The leaf-shattered sunlight reminded her of a print in the living room by Cézanne. "Cézanne," she said.

Antoine laid his hand on her shoulder and smiled.

Impressed? Teasing? Tolerant? She wanted him to take her hand.

They walked in silence, footsteps pressing the leaves and cracking the odd twig. They reached the lake and the earth became spongier. On the far side, teens were swimming and the female shrieks and shouts hinted at sex. Lorraine became self-conscious. They skirted the lake, a cool sheet of dark glass to their left, and reached a road. They crossed and started along a sidewalk when suddenly Antoine halted. A worm, writhing, caught part way across the hot cement. He picked it up and held it in his open palm. Like a tiny snake, it coiled and lashed.

"Okay, my friend."

Lorraine watched Antoine place the worm in the shade of a laurel hedge. They walked on. She'd never seen anyone do that. She realized that she too had spotted the worm, but had merely altered her step so as not to crush it, so as not to get any on her shoe.

"That was kind," she said.

"Have you ever been in the desert?"

"You know I haven't."

"I thought perhaps with Ray. In Las Vegas."

"No."

Antoine stopped again and this time closed his eyes and tilted his head back exposing his face to the sun. He stood there unselfconsciously, arms forgotten at his sides and face turned upward like a man stilled by an inner vision. A nearby lawn mower motor died. Lorraine looked. A few houses away a man watched them.

"You see things in the desert," said Antoine, eyes shut.

"Mirages?"

"Mirages in your mind."

Lorraine didn't know what he meant, but pretended she did. They walked on again, passing the man with the lawn mower who eyed them suspiciously. Enjoying the notoriety, Lorraine made a performance of nodding and smiling.

"Hello there!"

The man merely yanked the cord.

"What desert?" asked Lorraine.

"The Grand Erg Oriental. Algeria."

Algeria ... "When?"

"Oh ..." He gestured over his shoulder meaning a long time ago, back during the years he'd drifted.

The road crossed a railway cut. They leaned on the wide wooden railing right above the tracks. Lorraine envied all that travel, even the gesture dismissing it all. She wanted to live in obscure rooms in distant countries where entire streets are given over to markets — fruit, spices, silks — where goats eat the grass sprouting between the cobblestones, where the narrow streets have been walked for centuries, where there are mosques and temples instead of churches that look more like converted Safeway stores than places of worship. She thought of Jack attending school in the shade of date palms. She thought of hot rain, of walking hand-in-hand with Antoine through a field of lavender. She looked at him. He was frowning down at the tracks.

In the sunlight the rails burned as bright as glowing filaments. She smelled the creosote and tar. Leaning on her crossed fore-arms, she closed her eyes feeling the sun on her back, thinking she could stay like this for hours, that she was exactly where she wanted to be. Had she ever felt like this with Ray? The wooden railing began to vibrate, a tingling growing under her elbows. Both she and Antoine turned in time to see the engine loom into view with smoke balling from its stack. Now the entire bridge trembled and pigeons flapped up and the vibrating deepened so that Lorraine held on. When the train plunged beneath the bridge she was laughing as if on a carnival ride. Then the engine emerged directly below them, steel wheels screeling and racketing and the smoke rising. It was a long train. The engine was out of sight around the bend and the cars continued to pass. Boxcars, con-tainer cars, flatcars, cattle cars — the cows crowded and terrified, their heads bobbing like boats in a crowded cove.

Lorraine turned to Antoine and to her shock saw him cling-ing to the rail as if to a cliff, eyes clenched, shaking his head side to side.

"Antoine!"

But when she reached out to him he knocked her hand away and staggered off back the way they'd come. She followed, thinking he must be motion sick from the vibrations, or that he was coming down with something, that he was having a stroke or a spell.

"Antoine!"

He crossed the street. She caught up with him on the trail by Rain Lake. They walked along in silence, until whatever it was had passed and he sighed and apologized.

"Too much sun."

"Yes," she'd quickly agreed. "It's hot. Much better here under the trees."

❈

The music was so faint that at first Jack thought he was only remembering it. The Dickie Dee man. The piano music plunky-plunk-ka-plunk-a-plunk inside his ear. It always arrived unexpectedly. The kids would halt where they were — mid-step, mid-game, mid-shout — and race home for the nickels, dimes, or whatever change their mothers found in their purses or in ashtrays on windowsills.

Seated on the stool in the corner, Jack's head swivelled toward the window where he saw the ice-cream man in his tiny three-wheeled freezer truck, Fudgsicles and cones and bars dancing on the side. The entire class watched him motoring slowly along the street. Even Mr. Gough looked. Was it possible that he'd let them go get ice cream? And even as Jack watched, Mr. Gough strode toward the window as if he meant to call out to the Dickie Dee man. Instead he tugged the window shut. He went on down the row and tugged all the windows shut. The truck passed out of sight and the music faded. Mr. Gough turned. He looked right at Jack, who sucked a breath and swung around to face the corner again. He could feel his breath coming back at him off the walls. To be the Dickie Dee man was right up there with

Jack's dream of being a garbage man.

The last time he'd got ice cream from the Dickie Dee man Ivor and Nadia had been there. They all got chocolate, and in seconds Nadia's was smeared over her cheeks and chin and nose and even dribbling down her neck into her blouse. She groaned as she licked. She had the longest tongue Jack had ever seen. Her lips were thick and red and her skin smooth and white and her tongue was amazing. Jack didn't know how it fit in her mouth. She'd groaned the way she groaned there in the bush today with Mr. Skog.

That was also the way she'd groaned on the grass by Antoine's door. It was back at the start of the summer holidays. Antoine had his door open and was playing gypsy music on his hi-fi when Nadia appeared in the yard. She was wearing a lumberjack shirt and chewing on the end of a lock of her long red hair. She stood there, not moving, not saying anything, then she raised her arms and began to twirl. Jack was sitting on the porch steps eating Cap'n Crunch. Nadia shut her eyes and whirled with her head tilted and her arms out. She whirled and she whirled and soon Antoine was standing on the grass watching her.

He smiled and asked her, "Are you a gypsy?"

She began a droning moan and instead of whirling in one spot she danced around the yard. Jack thought she was playing airplane, dipping and swooping like a dive bomber. Then she tripped on one of the plum tree's roots and lay on her back with her arms out as if she meant to flap them up and down to make an angel in the snow.

"I'm Gypsy Rose Lee and I'm under a tree," she said.

Jack looked from Nadia to Antoine. Nadia was wearing cut-offs and the bottoms of her bare feet were black. The record ended and Antoine went inside and a few seconds later a new record came on. Symphony music. Jack recognized it from *Loony Toons and Merry Melodies* on TV. Antoine returned and Nadia sat up, legs out and mouth open, reminding Jack of Baby Huey. The music was louder now and Nadia closed her eyes and opened her mouth wider as if to hear better. She didn't moan as she had to the gypsy music, she just sat there very still as if she were watching cartoons on the insides of her eyelids. Then Antoine went to her and took her hands and she stood and they danced, very slowly, very gracefully, and when it was over Antoine bowed to her.

Jack now shut his eyes. But there was no Bugs Bunny or Daffy Duck or Roadrunner on the inside of his eyelids, only the kids and Mr. Gough behind him and the corner in front of him.

"Jack."

Jack's eyes jumped open.

"You're not there to sleep. You're there to think. Twenty-five-cent question! What is Jack there to think about?"

The class said nothing.

"Skog."

Jack waited for Ivor's answer.

"Being late."

"Being late," repeated Mr. Gough. "Did you hear that, Jack?"

The walls swam before Jack's eyes. He felt his voice vibrate back at him when he answered, "Yes."

"Good." Then Mr. Gough added, "Skog! There may be hope for you yet."

✶

Lorraine slid the matching suitcase from the shelf in the bedroom closet and began throwing clothes in. She twisted off her wedding ring and slapped it down by the photo of Ray's graduating class on his bedside table. She ran to Jack's room and got clothes for him. As she packed, she planned: grab Jack from school, then head for the airport. Vancouver to Montreal, then Montreal to Paris. Jack was young. He'd adapt. Jack would become Jacques.

The suitcases were the brand new kind with little wheels. Ray had ordered them from a catalogue. He'd slapped his forehead and cursed himself for not patenting the idea of putting wheels on suitcases himself.

Lorraine left the house as quickly as possible. Fearing Olivia would spot her, she looked neither right nor left and coached herself to keep her head down and just walk faster if Olivia called out. The suitcases — one with the money and one with the clothes — rolled easily down the sidewalk click-thumping like railcars at each seam in the cement. Train. Escape. *The Great Escape*. Ray had taken her and Jack to the Coronet to see it and she'd fallen in love with Steve McQueen on his motorcycle. All three of them had. They'd whistled the theme together. If only there'd been more of that.

She crossed the street and kept going. It occurred to her that the police would inevitably discover Antoine's identity. Was

Interpol tracing him? Would they want to talk to her? She recalled the news about Albert Schell waiting to stand trial for war crimes. She passed Winston Begbie's store and spotted Egbert Skog seated on a crate lighting matches. He lit them, then threw them down as if plucking petals from a flower, *She loves me, she loves me not.* Did Ray love Charlene? Did Charlene love Ray? Antoine loved you, Eva had said. A sob burst from Lorraine like a sneeze.

She reached the corner of Victoria and Kingsway breathless and sweaty, wiping tears from her cheeks. Her ringless finger felt strange and tingly. There was Rat Gardecki's gas station and Rat himself in that goofy green uniform and Barney Fife hat. Lorraine knew Rat would get a lot of mileage out of seeing her with suitcases. He and Olivia would pick it to the bone. To hell with him, to hell with them both. The light turned green and she walked, suitcases bouncing like wave-buffeted boats as she crossed the tire-rippled tarmac. She had to keep going. If you stop you'll sink, she counselled herself. Stepping up onto the curb she heard a horn.

"Lorraine!"

Ray. Across the street going in the other direction. She watched him U-turn and swing alongside as if docking a boat. The Thunderbird was so low he had to look up as he leaned across, wrinkling his forehead beneath his crewcut. She saw him swallow, that big Adam's apple sliding up and down making her think of a snake with an egg in its throat.

"Where you going?"

Lorraine watched him watch her. She saw the two of them here on the street and knew Rat Gardecki was probably on the phone to Olivia this very moment narrating it all like breaking news, and hearing, in turn, all about Antoine committing suicide. What now? Lorraine thought. She felt her arm float up on its own, but instead of aiming an accusing finger, instead of announcing she was leaving him, instead of stating she'd had it with his house and his car and his whore, she found herself pointing down the road to the small innocuous shops and houses lining the slow curve of Kingsway. "The Sally Ann. Getting rid of some old clothes."

Ray looked where she'd pointed and then looked at her. "Clothes?"

"Things I don't need." She shrugged. "It's a nice day. I wanted to walk." And even as she said it she heard the absurdity. Antoine was dead, her husband was having an affair. It was not a nice day, it was the worst day of her life. She watched Ray's eyes pinball from hers to the suitcases and back again. So, he'd come looking for her. He'd phoned and she hadn't answered and he'd panicked. She felt her spine strengthen. She felt satisfaction in the knowledge that he'd come running. He'd jumped out of Charlene's bed and driven home. She imagined yo-yoing Ray up and down, imagined him dangling on a string at her command. *No more living in a box, Ray. I've outgrown you, it's time to take me seriously.*

"Get in."

He shoved the door open toward her.

She didn't move. She bit her lower lip and considered her options. Airport? Flight? Jack in the seat next to her asking awkward questions? That terrified her. Returning to the old routine terrified her. It felt as if she was standing on a ledge. Jump or retreat?

"Come on."

She heaved the suitcases into the car, but stayed where she was. She wanted a rye and seven. Maybe they should go to a lounge and have a drink? She'd tell him about the money. It would snap Ray out of his rut; he'd looked at her and see *her* again. They'd sit close and whisper, make plans, just the two of them, like in a movie, Bogart and Bacall.

"Well?"

Lorraine was still on the sidewalk. She'd have to be madder than her mother to tell him about the money. And anyway, she couldn't let him see the gold fillings and gold teeth. She couldn't let anyone see them. Ever. It would only make it all worse. She'd bury them in the Jewish section of the cemetery. A ritual. Something decent.

"You gonna stand there forever?"

"What?"

"You gonna stand there?"

She got in but left the door open.

Ray waited, watching her.

She did nothing.

As Ray leaned across her thighs to tug the door shut she averted her face. He threw the Bird into gear and pulled out. Lorraine glanced off to her right and saw Rat Gardecki wiping a dipstick and watching them. She wondered if she should wave.

Then she gazed straight ahead and asked herself why she'd lied, and even as she wondered she knew the answer: because of fatigue, because he'd talk her out of it anyway. He'd get analytical; he'd start at the beginning, one, two, three, unscrewing the situation and taking it apart like one of his machines, examining each piece, then reassembling them in whatever order served him best. He always talked her out of things. He talked her out of driving lessons and out of going to university and out of going to France. If she showed him the money he'd probably pay off the mortgage or put it all down on a new house. As they drove, Lorraine stared out at the world from inside her skull.

And if she just took the money and left? If she took Jack and escaped to Europe or South America, what then? Jack would have no father and no friends. Would he blame her? Hate her? Didn't Lorraine blame her mother when her father was the one who ran off? Was that what Antoine meant with the money and the photo? Freedom had a price? Anyway, what would she do in South America? Sit in a room in Buenos Aires with her confused son? Would she be able to pick up the language? Would she be able to find a job? What about men?

She remembered the boys who'd tormented her after her mother went into the asylum. She remembered one of her afternoon meanders with Jack when he was still an infant. A man got on the bus and sat in the seat behind her whispering lewd come-ons. When she got off he followed and continued talking filth. He stayed just close enough to be heard, but not close enough to look like he was harassing her. Lorraine had been heading for Stanley Park but, frightened at the thought of entering the forest, turned back and hailed a cab.

She'd wanted to travel with Antoine *and* Jack as a sort of trio, a family. After all, what did she know of the world? Communists in Vietnam and Russia and Cuba, war in Algeria, war in Pakistan, revolution in the Congo and only weeks ago race riots in Los Angeles — right there on the cover of *Life* magazine, thirty-six dead.

"What happened?" asked Ray.

So, he wasn't even going to deny it. Lorraine leaned her head out the window and let the breeze cool her face. The breeze cleared the smell of cologne and liquor and cigarettes. Mostly, it cleared Charlene's perfume. He hadn't even washed it off.

"Heart attack?"

"Suicide."

"Jesus!" Ray thumped the steering wheel. "In our basement? The bastard! The filthy — it's like puking and leaving it for someone else to clean up."

Lorraine spoke quietly, "I'd have thought you'd be relieved."

"Oh! Yeah! Thanks! Mr. Ogre. That's me." Ray hunched hard over the wheel. "Hell, I am relieved. Saves me the trouble of going down there and doing it myself. Don't have to get my axe dirty."

Lorraine watched the road and read the signs: Susie's Beauty Salon, Driftwood Inn, Beaver Lumber and Supplies, Ray's Shoe-Re-New, Lobban's Flower Shop. Antoine was dead and Ray was having an affair. Did he bring her flowers? Little gifts? Lorraine turned and faced him. "Hey, Ray."

"What?"

"Fuck you!" She shrieked so loudly the words grated her throat.

Ray's shoulder jerked up and his head shrank into his collar. "I'm sorry."

"You bastard!"

His knuckles whitened on the wheel. "All right. All right!"

"You fuck."

Ray hated hearing Lorraine swear. "Jesus, don't swear."

"Fuck you."

"I'm sorry."

"Fuck you you're sorry."

"It just happened."

"Sure. Mr. Spontaneous." Trembling, she shut her eyes. She wanted to be far away, on a boat on the ocean, just the sun, the wind and the water. She realized she'd never been on a boat, not once. She opened her eyes, amazed at this fact. She said nothing for a while, then she said, "What do you think he's doing, Ray?"

"Who?"

She felt him look at her. She smiled bitterly and shook her head. Typical.

"Jacko?"

"First day of school." She could feel guilt boring its way into Ray's heart like a worm and she was glad. She hoped it hurt. She imagined Jack in a desk in the classroom and that guy, that teacher, Guff.

"One times one is one. How should I know?"

"You know everything else. You know Charlene."

"Come on ..."

"Is it good, Ray? Is she hot?"

"I told you, I'm sorry."

"Oh, did you tell me you were sorry, Ray? Gee, guess I didn't hear you. Thanks. All better now."

"Shit."

"Yup. There's a lot of that around." She propped her elbow on the window ledge and leaned her forehead in her hand.

Ray twisted the steering wheel as if trying to snap it. "How long was he dead?"

"I didn't ask, Ray. And they didn't privilege me with that information." From the corner of her eye she saw him shake his head, as if she was the unreasonable one.

After a while he asked, warily, "How the hell old was he?"

Lorraine heard her own flat voice. "Sixty." She felt Ray evaluating this information.

"Premier Bennett's sixty-five today."

Lorraine's lips twisted as if she'd bitten a lemon peel. Well, well. Ray had decided the crisis had passed. "Simple as that, eh, Ray?"

"I'm just saying —"

"Sure. What's the big deal?"

"I told you —"

"Just a little —" her hand fluttered up, " — piece on the side."

"Look —"

"She give you what you want?"

Ray said nothing.

"What *do* you want, Ray?"

He got smaller.

"Come on, Ray. Tell me."

He concentrated on his driving.

Lorraine found herself calculating: in forty-one years she too would be sixty-five; Ray would be eighty and Jack would be forty-seven. The year would be 2005. She tried imagining the year 2005. Plastic breasts, plastic skin, plastic clothes, Russia ruling the world. She thought of Antoine's photo in the envelope. No. She shut that door in her mind. She barred and locked it and chanted to herself: Her dad was a lad and her mother was mad, but me, I'm going to be free ...

Or maybe she'd get a hammer and beat those gold teeth into a bar and cash it in and no one would know. Teeth torn from human jaws. Teeth pried from gassed corpses. Antoine with a rifle. Tears burned their way like acid down her cheeks. If Antoine was here she'd slap him.

"Where's your ring?"

Ray sounded casual, but she could tell he was terrified. He feared she was leaving, feared finding his ring in the garbage. "I was scrubbing the sink."

Ray nodded as if that was a wise precaution.

The skin on her ring finger felt like grass unbending after the winter. The ring had changed her life. When people saw it on her finger she'd become a new and more mature person. But seven years later she knew the ring and the marriage and the baby hadn't really changed anything.

Ray swung the Bird into the Sally Ann parking lot and looked for a spot. He passed spaces that Lorraine knew he judged too narrow and endangered the car's paint. When he found two open spots next to each other he pulled in occupying both. He looked at her. "Jacko wasn't, he didn't see, did he?"

"Yup."

"He did?"

"Close enough to touch him."

Ray's face went waxy. "Is he all right?"

"Dandy, Ray, dandy."

Ray's chin dimpled and for a moment Lorraine thought he might cry. She didn't want to see him cry. She didn't have the energy or interest to deal with it. She got out.

"Let me," he said.

"No." She got both suitcases herself.

"I'll come with you."

"Don't bother." She impressed herself with her finality.

"You sure?"

"Uh-huh."

"I'll be right here," he called. "Okay?"

She started walking. "Fine."

✳

Ray watched her head for the double glass doors, thumped the steering wheel again then lit a cigarette and went over everything from the moment she'd gotten into the car. He'd given it away acknowledging he knew about Gaudin. Should he have played innocent? Could he have pulled it off? He exhaled smoke that hit the windshield and spread out and came rolling back to sting his eyes. He didn't want her to leave. He remembered the night his mother died. He didn't want to be alone again. What scared him was he suspected Lorraine was able to be alone, that she could cope. He never really knew what Lorraine was thinking. Over the years she'd gone from quiet and enigmatic to sarcastic and secretive. Her mind was always working something over, always churning something up, like a paddlewheel bringing the mud to the surface.

Ray sucked so hard on his cigarette it crackled like a brush fire. He smoked it to the filter, then lit another one. The ashtray was overflowing. He opened the door and dumped the butts onto the tarmac. He got out of the car and paced, thinking about how he'd break the news to Charlene: it had been great, she was wonderful, she was fabulous, at another time and in another place she'd have been the one, but it had to stop.

The cigarette smoke seared his throat. He watched the traffic: Chev, Buick, VW, Valiant. He thought of Schell and the crowd at that rally downtown. He'd never seen such a thing. Not even after the Lions won the Grey Cup last year. What kind of people were out in the middle of the afternoon like that? Hippies? Welfare bums? Agitators? What were they doing? He squatted by the front left tire and with his ignition key began picking pebbles from the tread. The smell of rubber made him think of Jacko seeing Gaudin's corpse. Six years old and facing a dead body in the basement. Shit. Jack had liked the old bugger. Ray remembered his father's corpse and his brother Del's in the hospital. Del — Jesus, the little runt had worshipped him. That was another reason he wanted Jack to have a kid brother, to know the blind adulation only a younger brother gave, to know what it was to feel protective. He'd seen his mother dead on the couch next to the old Marconi, sitting upright as if still listening to the newscaster reporting the progress of the Nuremburg tribunal. *Ma?* He'd touched her shoulder and she'd toppled sideways onto a cushion, a little plume of dust puffing like a last breath. *Ma!*

❖

Lorraine breathed the Sally Ann's stale air and looked for another exit, a loading dock, a side door, anything. There, through an archway, she spotted red block letters: XIT, the "E" burned out. She trundled her suitcases past a clerk who lowered her chin and studied her overtop of her rhinestone glasses. Lorraine passed a rack of men's suits, passed T-shirts, a shelf of *National Geographic* magazines. She went into the next room where the smells deepened. Shoes, brogans, slippers, skates, cleats, hockey pads. She continued on into furniture, where old oak and mahogany tables had been dumped in favour of tube metal and Formica. The suitcase wheels whirred and tripped on the curled seams of the lino. There it was: XIT.

She let go of one suitcase, straight-armed the metal bar and opened the double door. Sunlight. Air. Blackberries engulfing a wood fence. Lorraine reached back for her suitcase — but it wasn't there. She turned and found herself facing the clerk with the rhinestone glasses.

"Have you got a sales receipt?"

Lorraine didn't follow. "For what?"

"For these."

"They're mine."

Another clerk limped toward them.

"Yours?" said the first.

"Receipt, please," said the second. She drew herself up to as imposing a height as her crippled limb allowed.

"I'm just walking through." Lorraine stared at her suitcase in the clerk's hand. It was the one with the cash. Lorraine looked past her, through the archway to the entrance, expecting Ray any moment.

"She can't just walk through here," said the crippled woman with outrage in her voice. It was the voice of someone with a lifelong gripe, the voice Lorraine's mother used when talking about men. "She can talk to the police."

Lorraine lunged for her suitcase but the lame woman was rat-quick. She stepped between and blocked Lorraine. They were so close Lorraine smelled her coffee breath and saw the pores in her nose.

"Please."

"Why did you bring it in here?" said the other one. She wore a tight black sweater and her glasses had a silver string that looped across her bosom.

"She stole them both," said the lame one. "It's always the ones who don't need it who steal." She looked Lorraine up and down like she'd seen it before.

"There!" Lorraine pointed to the nametag clipped to the suitcase's handle. "Lorraine Klein. That's me. My name. On the tag."

The clerk in the glasses read the nametag. Her manner changed. "That's right."

But the other wouldn't give in. "She read it when she stole it."

"Do you have ID? A driver's licence?"

"No."

"You must have something."

She searched her wallet, embarrassed by her trembling fingers, but all she could find was a library card. The two clerks studied it.

Lorraine slowly reached out and took her suitcases. As she backed out the door, the crippled woman said, "The world's full of people like you." She yanked the door shut.

Lorraine found herself in a dead-end alley, corralled by the Sally Ann wall and the blackberry-covered fence. She considered heaving the suitcases over the fence and then climbing after them, but there were the blackberry thorns and barbed wire on top. Nowhere else to go, she rounded the corner of the building and saw the Thunderbird but no Ray. Her breath quickened. She glanced around. He must be in the store. She still had a chance. Then he appeared, stood up as if he'd been hiding by the front tire.

He opened his arms wide in a big shrug. "Well?"

She didn't know what to do so chucked the suitcases into the back, got in the car and sat there with her arms crossed.

✄

Ray guided the Bird into the carport and they went straight to Gaudin's door. Before opening it Ray looked at Lorraine.

"He's not, I mean, they took him away, right? I mean, you know, wouldn't want Jacko walking in."

"He's at school. First day. Remember? Oh, but I guess you were kind of busy. You had other things on your mind, eh?"

Ray exhaled hard and said nothing. What could he do but roll over and expose his belly? "What happened to all those birds?"

Lorraine looked up at the plum tree.

Ray followed her gaze. The tree was full of canaries.

Lorraine thought of a medieval tapestry, a tree thick with strange fruit and mythological birds. They'd all be eaten by hawks, isn't that what Antoine had said?

Ray tucked his chin and cleared his throat. As he opened the door he took a big breath and, cringing, stepped on in. Something crunched underfoot and he jumped. Birdseed. He looked around. No blood, no damage, no sign of struggle or crisis, just the yellow dishcloth hung neatly across the gooseneck faucet and the drawers all shut. The room smelled of bird pee, guano, damp seed and something else. The six wire cages stood open. "Where was he?"

Lorraine's hand pointed limply to the couch.

Ray stayed back. "How?"

"I don't know."

"Poison?"

"I said I don't know!"

"Okay, okay."

"Cyanide."

"Cyanide?"

Lorraine nodded and dropped into a chair at the kitchen table, put her elbow on it and leaned her head on her palm. When Ray looked at her she looked right back at him, not realizing she was doing it. She was imagining him having sex with Charlene. She'd seen Charlene and knew she was stacked. Did Ray say he loved her? Was it a furtive fuck, or a long and languid lovemaking with music and wine and candles? Maybe Charlene wanted him to run away with her. Where would a woman — a broad — like Charlene want to run away to? But the answer was obvious: Las Vegas. Lorraine began to cry.

"It's okay." Ray stepped toward her, yet she rushed by him out of the room.

Ray plodded after her up the wooden steps and into the kitchen. "Lor?" He went to the bedroom but the door was shut and locked. "Lor?" No answer. He checked his watch. One. He went to the can where he washed his face and looked in the mirror. He was sweating again and his shirt — the second of the day — was soaked. Not only that, it smelled of Charlene's perfume ... He put the heel of his hand to his forehead. How could he have been so sloppy? He might still have lied his way out of it. But even as he thought that he saw how stupid it was. Lorraine knew. She'd phoned. She'd put it together. Ray forced himself to evaluate the situation. There was nothing to do but go to the office, re-establish routines, act as normal as possible. He didn't want to lose her and he certainly couldn't bear losing Jacko. First day of school. He should have dropped him off there himself, had a little man-to-man at the start of the big day. There'd never be another first day of school.

Now was the time to agree to that holiday in France. Start planning it for the spring. Why not? And in that moment he even smiled, his heart hopping at the thought of getting on a plane. Why had he put up such a fuss? He returned to the bedroom door and knocked lightly. "Lor? Lor, it's not what you think." He waited for her to respond. "Hey, how about we take that trip? You know, to France?"

"Go back to work, Ray."

16
Aladdin's Lamp

Each time Jack's knees began bouncing or he glanced at the window, Mr. Gough touched him with the yardstick, lightly but seriously, in both a warning and a reminder. Jack's mind wandered into all manner of horror. Was his mother wrong? Was this one of those boarding schools he'd seen on TV where the kids slept in one big room and never left except for one day a year? Fists clenched between his knees, Jack stared into the corner where the two walls met and listened to the clock-like tick of Mr. Gough's shoes as he paced side to side in front of the class.

Jack thought of the alarm clock his dad had given him. The

clock had two bells that looked like ears and a key on the back that made a grinding sound when you cranked it. His dad taught him how to set the alarm, but the clock was gone now and Jack blamed that book from the library. Every Saturday morning Jack's mother took him to the library and he got books. One was a joke book.

What time is it when an elephant sits on the fence?

Time to get a new fence.

Ha ha ha.

And there was this joke, too, the joke he blamed: Two boys stand facing each other. One boy holds an alarm clock. He says to the other boy, "Want to see time fly?" The other boy says, "Yes." So the first boy throws the clock out the window.

Ha ha ha.

The afternoon Jack made time fly the clock shattered on the sidewalk and lay like a dead bird.

Would Antoine's canaries still be there in the tree or would they have flown off? The day Antoine moved in, Jack carried one of the birdcages. The canaries' whirring wings made the same sound as when he clipped a baseball card to his bicycle spokes. Antoine had invited Jack in and shifted a chair so he could stand on it and study the birds. All winter long Antoine invited Jack in and they watched the birds and played checkers. When winter ended, Antoine used to take a chair outside and tip it back against the wall and enjoy the sun. He showed Jack how to make shadow figures with your hands: rabbit, fox, bat, Luger.

Now Jack saw his own shadow on the wall. By turning his

head even a little he changed the shape of his shadow. There it was — his face — *him*, as if there were two Jacks, one in here and one out there, like brothers. Or was one a good Jack and one a bad Jack? He'd never thought of that before, just as he'd never thought of boy letters and girl letters. He frowned and saw the shape of his brow changed too.

And what if Antoine wasn't sick but dead? What did dead mean? Jack knew there was heaven and there was hell for when you were dead, so dead meant going somewhere else. Jack and his parents had gone on holidays for one week at the beginning of July. They'd gone to a house on the beach that had spiders in the rafters and no hot water. Jack's mother hated it and later told Olivia Edson that it was just hell there. Maybe Antoine had gone to a place like that, or maybe Jack would find him in his basement suite this afternoon, feeling much better thank you very much, and Jack would help him herd all the birds back into their cages. Usually in the afternoon Antoine let the canaries fly about the room. Antoine would hold out his arms and they'd perch on them as if he were a tree. "Someday I'll have so many canaries they'll pick me up and take me for a ride." Jack liked that. He'd spread his arms, too. He and Antoine would stand facing each other with their arms out amid the flapping birds, Jack pleading silently, "Please, please, land on me and take me for a ride." Lately, some of them did come and land on his arms. They whirred about his head like angels and then perched on him, their claws gripping his skin right through his shirt, their faint weight like nothing at all. When that happened Antoine coached him, talking without moving his mouth, like a ventriloquist.

"Don't turn your head, Jack. That's it, breathe easy and smile, birds like it when you smile."

And so he smiled and the canaries trusted him and lined themselves up along his arms and it was like he was growing feathers and turning into a bird himself.

✸

"Since most of you are new to school, this entire first week you will have an afternoon recess," announced Mr. Gough.

Jack felt the relief that rippled through the room. He heard Mr. Gough go to the door and oversee the ceremonial departure of the kids from the class. When Ivor Skog attempted to leave, Gough stopped him and said, slowly, in a voice of genuine confusion, "Skog, what has happened to your hair?" In the silence that followed, Jack knew Mr. Gough was examining Ivor's stick-stiff quills. "You're going to be a big problem, Skog, a two-dollar problem. But I will solve you. You have my promise."

"Thank you," said Ivor. Then added, quickly, "Sir."

From the stool in the corner Jack could tell when it was just him and Mr. Gough left in the room. Jack's stomach hurt. He thought of the rag his mom wrung after doing the dishes. He heard Mr. Gough sigh. Hands clenched between his knees, Jack's palms sweated. His time had come. He had to walk the plank. Yet Mr. Gough said nothing. Was this what they meant by the silent treatment? Would he get the strap? Would Mr. Gough beat him with the yardstick?

Finally Mr. Gough said, "A new era has begun, Jack. A new era. Your life has taken a turn. You're going to be in school a long time."

Jack heard Mr. Gough's footsteps approach and felt him come to a stop right behind him.

"The essence of school is limits, Jack. You must learn those limits. Because life has limits. You want to be prepared for life, don't you, Jack?"

Jack watched Mr. Gough's shadow on the wall. Mr. Gough's shadow was so big it swallowed Jack's shadow. Then he felt Mr. Gough grip the stool and dial him around so that they were face to face. Mr. Gough had crouched so as to be eye level. "Eh, Jack?"

Jack nodded, not because he agreed or knew what Mr. Gough was talking about, but because he knew Mr. Gough wanted him to agree. The pores on either side of Mr. Gough's nose were deep, there was dandruff in his eyebrows and the veins in his eyes looked like red barbed wire. Mr. Gough had barbed wire in his eyes. Again Jack nodded.

"Good. Now, off you go."

Jack fled past him into the hall.

"Walk!"

Jack forced his legs to go slowly. Up ahead he saw a door with a stick figure on it. The washroom. He needed to pee. He'd been holding it back since lunch. Pushing open the door, cold odours thumped him in the nose. Snickering Grade Sevens huddled around one of the sinks. Jack recognized them; they were the ones who'd been kicking each other out on the field. He scooted wide around them and stepped up to the metal trough that was littered with lumps of gum and white hunks of urinal disc.

As he unzipped his corduroys and tweezed out his diddles he listened to the Grade Sevens.

"Tear it, you're dead, Nickerson."

"Not too full."

"It's a blue boob!"

Nervous at the proximity of the Grade Sevens, Jack was only just beginning to relax enough to start peeing when the boys turned.

"Hey, kid."

Jack looked.

"Think fast."

The lobbed water balloon wobbled through the air in an arc so high Jack had to cock his head back to follow its slow-motion trajectory as it rose then hovered then fell. Only at the very last instant did he react. As he did he lost his footing on the slick tile. The balloon splatted him in the face as he fell hard, whacking his hip, elbow and head and ending up with one arm right in the urinal trough while the Grade Sevens fled.

✄

When Jack pulled open the main door, a blaze of pain shot up his elbow and the sunlight blinded him. He faced a world of silver shapes that swirled and shouted. As his eyes adjusted he saw kids wheeling in packs about the schoolyard. He started down the cement steps, hurt hip making him limp, goose-egged head throbbing. He'd washed his arm and dried his shirt with toilet paper. His only thought was, Don't cry. He stood by the red brick wall feeling its heat against his back. The heat felt reassuring. He slid slowly down until he was sitting in the dirt. Everyone was running. Ivor was running. Miriam was running. Even Fat Boy Burton who had breasts like a lady that jiggled under his shirt, was running. Pressing himself to the hot brick, Jack watched the world out there on the other side of his eyes. Grade Ones peeled apart their sandwiches and threw the bread in the air, popped their paper bags, stomped oranges, coughed milk out their noses, smashed their apples to the ground or threw them at the seagulls and crows crying and cawing overhead. Ivor had Fat Boy Burton by the back of the gonch and was pulling.

✄

Lorraine stayed in the bedroom until Ray left, then she emerged and wandered the house, eventually coming to a halt before the globe. She shut her eyes and gave it a spin, and when the globe stopped she reached out and touched it. France. Ray had said they'd go to France, but Lorraine didn't want to go to France with Ray. What she wanted — what she *needed* — was a place to hide the money. And the place, she realized, was right in front of her: the globe itself. It had two halves that screwed together at the equator. She lifted the globe from its stand, then held the southern hemisphere between her knees and twisted the northern. When the globe was two metal bowls she got the suitcase and dumped all the notes into one of them and screwed the halves back together and remounted it. She gave it a spin. Silence. At any rate, it would do for the time being. But what about the teeth? She picked the sack up — sickeningly heavy — and dropped it onto the coffee table. It hit with a smack.

She fixed a rye and seven and drank it in front of the globe. All those countries: France, Germany, Belgium, Spain. She thought of Antoine and she thought of those teeth. She turned and looked at the sack. She fixed another drink, then lay down on the couch. The sack of teeth lay within reach on the coffee table. She got up and paced by the far wall. She had to make plans. She had to be ready — but for what? To ruin Jack's life by depriving him of a father? She thought of the rainy afternoon she found Ray in the alley with Jack, both of them in their gumboots and hats, splashing about up to their shins, laughing and shouting as they battled the raging water, building a dam of stones and boards and mud.

Now that Lorraine had the means to leave, France with its landmines, Vietnam with its war, Africa and South America with their revolutions, New York with its murders and Los Angeles with its riots weren't so attractive. More importantly, how would she survive without Antoine? Look at her mother. She went mad when the man she loved left her — when the man she loved abandoned her. Lorraine realized that perhaps it wasn't that her mother was so weak, but that her love had been so strong that when the bond was broken so was she.

Two drinks in her, she stepped onto the porch and surveyed the yard and the houses and in the distance, the bush surrounding Rain Lake. She didn't want to end up like her mother. She didn't want to end up like Olivia Edson or Eva Skog. She returned to the living room and got the sack.

She went down the steps and down the alley and kept walking. When she reached the bush she followed the trail on in — the same trail she and Antoine had walked that strange Sunday morning — descending into the smells of mulch and cottonwoods, ripe blackberries and undergrowth. The glint of foil from a cigarette pack made her think of a coin. Knowing Jack loved everything about pirates, Antoine drew him a treasure map earlier in the summer. It showed a tropical island with palm trees, a ship at anchor, and a dotted line leading to buried treasure. He did a job worthy of a forger, using stiff paper whose edges he scorched and blackened, then rolled into a tube like a pirate chart. The map led to a treasure chest buried here in the bush. Jack spent days hunting it, digging holes with Ray's army shovel. He found the treasure buried in a McVitie's Shortbread tin and breathless with joy brought it home. It contained a checked cloth in which were tied three silver Spanish coins.

Her hand sweating, Lorraine gripped the sack tighter. The birds raced ahead from branch to branch like messengers. The deeper she went the stronger the smells of earth and leaves and cedar, and then there was the lake itself with its glassy surface and sweet boggy scent. In the middle it looked almost black, while closer to the edge it was the colour of tea. Dragonflies hovered over beer bottles bobbing like tiny buoys. She wandered the mossy perimeter, the ground spongy beneath her feet, the salal thick with dark blue berries, and she felt simultaneously weepy with relief at having escaped the house and devastated by the events of the day.

Soon her feet were soaked through her thin canvas shoes.
She didn't care. Antoine was gone; Ray was sleeping with
Charlene; her father was a myth. She found a raft nudged up
against the submerged grass. It was built of logs overlaid with
planks and about the size of their back porch. When she stepped
onto it the raft listed. She set the sack down and picked up the
pole and pushed off. Seeing the bottom fall away so suddenly,
she got scared and thought she should go back — but go back
where? She probed with the pole, a branch stripped of bark,
and found the bottom and pushed again. The water draped in
folds past the front of the raft and the shore receded. Each time
she pushed, the pole refracted and disappeared into the depths.
Soon she was far from the shore and the sun was hot and high
and the lake water cool. There was no wind and no sound but
for the water sliding and dripping from the pole. A fish jumped.
She tried to see it swimming but it vanished. As she worked
she felt the muscles tightening in her arms and thighs, the pole
solid in her grip, her entire body sinewy with reborn strength.
She remembered running when she was a kid, running and
jumping rope and throwing sticks. Starting to perspire, she
scooped water onto her face and neck and felt it run cool down
her neck and under her top between her breasts. Putting her
hand to her brow she scanned the lake and saw the trees looked
different from here, everything looked different.

She resumed pushing, as if she was Charon ferrying souls
across the Styx. Antoine was with her and so was her father.
She felt them nearby and knew she had to get them to the other
side. When the water was too deep for the pole she sat down

cross-legged and stared into a glassy well of sunlight descending deep into the lake. She could see her own reflection, could look right through it, and she knew what she had to do. She picked up the sack of teeth — its grim weight heavy in her hand — and reached back to throw it, then paused. Should she say some sort of prayer? She didn't know any prayers. She flung the sack as far from the raft as she could. It hit and sank and in seconds even the ripples were gone.

Ignoring the shore and anyone who might be watching, she peeled off her clothes. The sun and air felt good on her skin. Dangling her legs in the cool lake she felt the wet planks under her thighs. She gave a push and let herself slip into the water. It slid up and enclosed her like a skin. Submerged, her hair haloed her head like fine weed. Sun spears pierced her. She floated. There was the raft with its turnip-coloured logs. There was the sun in the other world. She exhaled and bubbles rushed to the surface while she sank, arms out, falling back and back with the water curling between her legs and under her arms.

She broke the surface and hoisted herself onto the hot planks and stretched out on her back. She thought of Ray who'd betrayed her, of her father who'd abandoned her, and of Antoine who'd rejected her. That left only Jack. Her skin tightened as the sun dried the water on her belly and thighs and forehead. She spread her arms and legs and let the sun do its work. After a while, with passengers to deliver to the far shore, she dressed, picked up the pole and using it as a paddle, continued on her way.

⌘

Halfway to work Ray changed his mind and headed to Charlene's. The rally had been cleared from the courthouse, but it was still slow going and the gas fumes rippled the air in a mirage of hoods and trunks and chrome.

Charlene was surprised to see him. Her eyes were wet and uncertain.

He kissed her and said, "I saw myself."

"You saw yourself."

"And I don't know."

"You don't know."

They sat in Charlene's kitchen overlooking Stanley Park and Lost Lagoon. Couples held hands and strolled the path that circled the lagoon, which was busy with geese and swans and ducks.

"I just ..."

Charlene watched as Ray's hand, lying on the tabletop, rose then dropped. Seated only four feet away, she felt as if she wasn't even in the same room — she couldn't be — she couldn't risk it, not anymore. She watched Ray begin to laugh, a bewildered shaking of the head.

"She's my wife," he said, as if he'd never realized it before.

"Your wife."

"Well, yeah." He looked up. Had Charlene forgotten that rather significant little fact? "It's like —" He gazed at the moon-shaped light fixture on the ceiling above the table. "Like I'd forgotten."

"You forgot."

He hoisted his shoulders in a big shrug.

Charlene pursed her lips and probed her cheek with her tongue. Ever since Lorraine's phone call she'd been anticipating something like this. She'd got herself dressed up as a sort of self-defence. She was wearing high-waisted red shorts, a white blouse, red button earrings and cork-soled sandals. The sandals were new and felt like she had Styrofoam on her feet. They made her feel like her feet weren't quite touching the ground. She'd bought them because they reminded her of a painting she'd seen of a Venetian woman crossing St. Mark's Square during an *aqua alta*, a high water, her platform shoes keeping her dry against the threat of the rising sea. She hadn't expected Ray to reappear like this. When he'd buzzed she'd been ready to weep with relief, her hope dancing ahead like a girl in a ballerina costume. But the little girl fell face first.

"We're going to go to France," said Ray.

"Good idea."

"You think so?"

"You know what, Ray?"

He looked at her innocently awaiting her advice. That was, after all, why he was here. "What?"

"I want a coffee. How about you run down to the corner and grab a bottle of cream?" She reached across the table and placed her hand on his hand, reassuring him that everything was fine.

"Sure." He smiled. Wanting to be helpful, he asked, "You got any empties?"

Charlene found two empty cream bottles under the sink.

Ray went out the door and along the carpeted hall that

smelled of movie theatre popcorn. That was the thing about Charlene. She was mature. She understood and she was still there for him. Hell, in Arab countries a guy could have four wives. All he wanted was two.

There was a kumquat tree in the window of the corner store. The place smelled of cool concrete, incense and fruit. An old Chinese guy sat smoking behind the ancient cash register. On a shelf, joss sticks fumed before a pyramid of oranges.

"Hot enough for you?"

Ray smiled and shook his head. "Eighteen days."

"Drought."

They both chuckled at the absurdity. Eighteen days and the radio wags were talking camels and sand dunes.

Ray strolled back up the sidewalk to Charlene's, swinging the bottle of cream, thinking it was all in how you looked at it. Antoine was dead. He felt bad about that. Down there all that time, obviously eaten up by something. Maybe he'd been wrong about the guy? Lorraine would take it hard, as would Jacko. So okay, France. It'd cost a bundle, but what the hell? He kicked a dandelion. His shoulders slackened and relaxed as he slowed down and admired the roses in front of Charlene's building. He leaned and gave them a sniff. The roses had a hint of raspberry. Tea roses. They'd had them by their house as a kid. His mother snipped them and made bouquets for the table. He wished his mother had lived to see Jack, that way he'd have a real grandmother, a proper grandmother.

Ray buzzed Charlene's number and waited. And the old man; he'd have liked Lorraine. France. Three weeks. Next May. Or who knows, maybe even sooner. October, when the leaves are changing. Old Paree. He buzzed again. Maybe she jumped in the shower. He inhaled deeply: sunburnt grass, roses, a hint of the lagoon from off through the trees. Goddamn it, he loved Vancouver. He could see the water dark and shiny in the afternoon sun. Above him, the wind shivered the maple leaves. He buzzed a third time. Nothing. He stepped onto the lawn and called up to her window, "Hey ..." Searching his pockets he found a penny and pitched it. It ticked the glass and dropped into the roses. He found two more pennies, then a nickel, then a quarter, then he didn't have any more coins.

⌘

When the bell rang Jack and the other Grade Ones returned to their seats in room 102.

Mr. Gough was manning the door and welcoming them back. He was smiling. He looked them over and said, "Good. All here and accounted for. Even Jack found his way back." There were titters. Mr. Gough was in a good mood again. Jack felt his cheeks burn with fear and confusion, and at the same time felt grateful that Mr. Gough let him return to his desk at the back of the row. Was he a two-dollar problem like Ivor? Would Mr. Gough solve him?

"Excellent. You're not the worst class I've ever had, in fact you might well prove to be one of the more interesting. It's all a matter of getting off on the right foot. Now, this afternoon we can loosen up a little. I'm going to teach you a song. You like songs, don't you?" Mr. Gough looked at them inquiringly and Jack saw some kids nodding so he nodded too.

"Good." He picked up his yardstick and held it like a conductor's baton. "The Happy Wanderer." He rapped the desk. "Listen!" And in a voice that surprised Jack because it was so fine and clear, Mr. Gough sang, "Oh, I love to go a-wandering along the mountain paths." He repeated the line twice more and each time Jack was transported despite the fact that he'd never been in the mountains.

"Now. Everybody," said Mr. Gough. "Oh, I love to go a-wandering along the mountain paths!" Together they all sang along. *Val-der-ee, val-der-aah, val-der-ee, val-der-ah ha ha ha, ha ha ha haaah,* their bird-like voices rising together in a shrill and uncomprehending chorus. Jack sang loudly and so did Fat Boy Burton and so did Miriam and even Ivor. Despite his goose-egged skull, Jack sang until the sound blocked everything else from his mind.

At three o'clock when school finally let out Jack felt older, as if he'd been away from his life for many years and now he was back. Clutching his Aladdin's lamp lunch box like a football, he ran along the hall past the washroom and up the stairs and burst into the afternoon light. Ivor was already outside gripping a younger boy in a headlock. Ivor grinned and waved Jack over.

"Jack!"

Jack ran for the gate in the chain-link fence at the far end of the field. Thinking of his mother and the globe, thinking of his dad and the Thunderbird, thinking of Antoine and his canaries, he ran faster. He ran despite his bruised hip and throbbing elbow and sore head. If Antoine was still sick, Jack would stand beneath the plum tree and hold out his arms; if he kept very still the canaries would come and land on him and he'd carry them back inside to their cages and Antoine would be happy.

He passed blackberry bushes thick with ripe fruit that normally he'd have eaten; he ran right on by a Coke bottle in a ditch. When he reached his alley he ran faster. The alley had been oiled earlier that summer to keep down the dust, but now the dust was there again, a parched black powder that smelled like Rat Gardecki's gas station. He reached his carport with its familiar smell of cool cement and old wood. As he cut through it he slipped on a patch of oil and his Aladdin's lamp lunch box clattered to the cement and broke open, but no genie smoked out to give him three wishes. He left the lunch box where it was and continued on through to his backyard and went straight to the basement suite door. It was open and canaries were flying in and out.

"Antoine!"

But he didn't find Antoine. What he found froze him. What he found made him fall back a step and raise his arm to shield his face. Egbert Skog was sleeping on the couch. Egbert Skog snored, mouth hanging slack, empty vodka bottle on the floor under the coffee table while the canaries pecked about the couch and on Egbert's arms and legs. The canaries whirled up when Jack burst into the room and some flew past him out the door. Terrified, Jack backed out and stood in the yard.

He stared at Egbert and then looked up at the plum tree where the rest of the birds were crying. Not knowing what else to do, he raised his arms the way he'd done before, the way Antoine had shown him. He held his arms out as if he too was a bird, and he waited. As he did the birds continued to shrill hysterically, shrieking like the steel wheels of a braking train.

Acknowledgements

Thanks to the B.C. Arts Council and The Canada Council, who both gave me money to complete this book. As well, thanks to *sub-TERRAIN* magazine who published a piece of this novel in the March 2002 issue.

Finally, thanks to Eden for inspiration and support.

About the Author

G rant Buday is the author of *White Lung* and *Monday Night Man*, both nominated for a City of Vancouver book award and optioned for feature films. His novella *Under Glass* was shortlisted for the Ethel Wilson Fiction Prize in 1995. He is also the author of *Golden Goa*, a travel memoir of India. Buday is a winner of the Western Magazine Award for Fiction.